Your Friend E

Anne Ousby

There's what I know
there's what you know
there's what they know
and then, there's the truth

Best Wishes

from Anne Ausby

The subject matter of 'Your friend E' has caused much debate and I want to thank everyone for their opinions and insights into what has been a difficult topic.

My heartfelt thanks go to Wendy, Gillian and Avril for inspiring me to write this book and helping me along the way. To Anne, Ali, Erica and Margaret for reading the book and making such insightful comments and to my long-suffering, eagle-eyed, editing gurus, Maureen and Brenda.

Your friend E

Dear V, Thinking of you. May God protect you from your friend E.
I left the comma out on purpose.

Sentencing - day one

'You've been here every day.'

    I wasn't sure who Terry Davey was talking to. He was sitting directly in front of me leaning forwards, like he always did. His usual companions sat with him - Thea, his niece, sitting close, and then Magda, his estranged wife, at a distance. Davey's eyes were fixed on the man in the dock - the man who murdered his daughter.

    No one else seemed to have heard him but me. Maybe I was dreaming - I was frightened of my dreaming - but Terry Davey was no phantom and after a moment he shuffled around until he was looking me straight in the eyes. There was no mistaking who he was talking to this time.

    'What are you? Journalist? Cop? One of his people?'

    The judge stopped in mid-sentence and looked up. Everyone was staring at us. Thea whispered to Davey, pulling at his sleeve, and eventually he turned away. When all was quiet again the judge continued. She was summing up and her soft monotone spun around the courtroom like a spider's web in the breeze.

I was fighting to keep my eyes open. Sometimes the words made sense, other times they drifted away into nothingness. It was important to hear every word and I sat up straighter and concentrated.

'Nothing I can say will change what happened to the deceased and her family...'

'Deceased?' What sort of a word is that? So clinical, so emotionless, so 'wet-wipe' squeaky clean. And how does any word convey the horror of that slaughterhouse we had all seen on the TV screens? The World knew what had happened to the beautiful, young Rachel Davey and *'Deceased'* didn't cover it.

'You've been here every day.'

For a moment I'd forgotten about the old man, but he hadn't finished with me, not yet. 'What d'you want?' His words were forced out between clenched teeth - his sad, yellowing old man's teeth. I shifted uncomfortably but there was nowhere to go. The women on both sides of me were ramparts pressing in on both sides. They knew I was the enemy.

Davey's face was close to mine now. Thea was doing her best to shut him up but he wouldn't let it go. He didn't give a toss if he was noticed. He had nothing else to lose.

'Get your kicks from all this, do you?'

His voice was cracked and raw as if each syllable was cutting his throat, and I smelt his skanky breath. *'Sicko,'* he spat at me. I looked into his red-rimmed, eyes. There was nothing there but pain. I don't know what he saw in mine. Then he started to

3

cough, great, harsh, rattling paroxysms that racked his body and left him breathless and swaying. Thea pulled him back to the front and he crumpled against her. I saw the flash of white as she pressed a handkerchief into his trembling fingers and he thumped down hard on the bench.

An usher passed some water to Davey. No wonder he couldn't breathe properly, the air in the courtroom was stifling. I could feel sweat trickling down my back. The air-con had broken down again and the fans did nothing but shunt the leaden air about the room, like pass the parcel - only no one wanted to get that particular parcel.

The judge called a twenty minute recess. The chief prosecutor grumbled that it would take more than twenty minutes just to clear the courtroom but I noticed he was one of the first to leave. I scrambled out of my bench, side-stepping journalists who squatted on the stairs, crouched over their tablets and I pushed between people standing shoulder to shoulder along the back walls. A lot of them stayed where they were, no doubt worried they would lose their places if they left the court. As I joined the queue shuffling out I looked for V - that's what I call Viktor Heiney.

He was in the dock on the other side of the court. Two policewomen flanked him and his family and friends sat behind. He wasn't a big guy but if I craned my neck I could just see his head. His sister, Melanie, looked up at that moment and when she caught my eye I smiled and held up crossed fingers. I was glad I'd

4

managed to send the box of my special truffles to them that morning. She saw me and nodded.

I looked around the courtroom. The Davey and Heiney families were separated by the stairs and the prosecuting and defence teams sat down in the well, facing banks of screens and towering stacks of files and books. The witness box stood to one side and then the polished benches reared up like a cresting wave. Two assessors (assistant judges) dressed in black, sat on podiums on either side of the pinnacle, where the judge perched. She was a diminutive scarlet bird, flaring like a flame. The Flame of Justice?

I'd studied this judge for over a year and a half and I still had no idea what she was thinking. Her expression and her demeanour never changed, however gruesome the evidence. She was always polite and never harangued the witnesses like some judges I'd seen. Press opinion was divided about her. All I knew was that she was incredibly fastidious and dissected every shred of evidence.

My two women companions were behind me in the queue to get outside and when I caught them looking at me they turned their backs. I was used to their hostility. They knew I supported the Heiney clan but they didn't know the half of it. I was V's best friend. I was E.

Once outside I found a quiet spot around the back of the building with the smokers. I kept my eyes down, concentrating on lighting my cigarette. I took the first soothing drag then leant against the wall, resting one foot behind me. I could hear the buzz of conversations around me. Someone was complaining about something. There was a lot to complain about in this trial.

I used the time tweeting Melanie. 'Tweeting'? A toy town word for a toy town concept. Before this I had never tweeted but now I saw its power. It was anonymous, it was instant, it was succinct. Tweeting was perfect for my needs and I'd been using it from day one, to forge a link between the Heiney clan and myself. They saw me in the courtroom every day and knew I was their friend but they didn't know I was the E who sent them gifts - not yet.

I'd had a result that morning. Melanie had tweeted asking if I was the person who'd sent V the lovely cushion and all the boxes of truffles? And, if I was, could we set up a meeting soon? She wanted to thank me in person. She also told me that Viktor sent his love, gratitude and God's blessing. '*He hopes you can meet in happier times.*' I replied, 'Yes, I'm *E and I would love to meet up, anytime.*'

There were other, more worrying things, to think about too. My savings were almost gone and I'd lost my job.

Dan kept texting me, leaving voice mails, tweets, messages on Face book, Skype, the whole twittering, tweeting, barrow-load of techno-geekery. His name popped up all over my phone screen. '*Where are you, Evie?*', '*Why don't you talk to me?*', '*Please, ring, I'm worried about you.*' But I didn't trust him. He was trying to set me up again. I had to keep focussed on the main event, I mustn't get side-tracked by Dan or anyone.

I was first in the queue to get back inside after the recess. I couldn't chance sitting behind Davey again in case we were ejected, so I had to find somewhere else. I looked everywhere but it was hopeless. In desperation I considered going to the press overflow area outside the courtroom; at least that way I could follow the summing up and sentencing on the link there. As I hesitated, someone touched my arm.

'Looking for somewhere to perch, honey? If you promise not to breath too much you can wedge yourself here.' A woman patted the couple of empty centimetres on the end of the bench she was sitting on.

I muttered, 'Brilliant, thanks,' and sat down. At least I could sit with my legs in the aisle.

'We've got to look after our own, haven't we?' She'd seen my press bracelet. 'Which paper?'

'Out of town weekly. you won't have heard of it.' I lied.

I recognised her. She was a big-shot crime reporter for 'The Cape Times.'

'Miserable old bastard?' she mouthed, looking down at Davey. I shrugged and she gave me a penetrating look. 'Don't I know you from somewhere?'

I shook my head.

'Umm,' she was still looking at me. 'Got it. You're Evie Adze aren't you?'

'No.'

She raised an eyebrow at me. 'Okay, maybe I'm wrong, but I'm usually good at faces.'

I bet you are, I thought, flicking on my cell, pretending to be busy. I could feel her eyes on me. I was sitting in a nest of journalists. They were all buzzing furiously away on their gizmos, but after a moment some of them lifted their heads, sniffing the air, sensing the woman's interest in me. Who was I? Was I someone worth following up? What was my story? Fortunately for me I have a forgettable face. Maybe it was growing up in the shadow of a beautiful sister that had made me so invisible? But I wasn't taking any chances and I would make sure I disappeared quickly at the end of the day's proceedings.

Shortly after this the judge returned and unexpectedly brought the session to a close. Possibly she thought it unwise to pass judgement when Terry Davey was in such a state, or perhaps she and the assessors couldn't reach a unanimous verdict? Whatever, the sentence was postponed until tomorrow. Another day to get through.

The beginning

From day one of the bail hearing the Viktor Heiney case had *fiasco* written all over it. Nothing was straightforward. The lead investigating detective had to be replaced after it was disclosed that he, himself, would be going to court soon, on corruption charges. Countless witnesses were called and dismissed as unreliable, points of law were debated, procedural cock-ups were argued about interminably. There were lengthy discussions between the prosecution and defence teams as to whether the trial should be televised and transmitted live and continual wrangles about the use of rolling footage from the courtroom. Scratch your bum or itch your nose and there you'd be in some repulsive close up on the News. But it wasn't all bad because this was how I got to see that V was using my cushion. The clip was shown on YouTube the first night of the bail hearing.

Ma said I'd never make a needle-woman - I was too impatient. But I think she'd have been impressed with my efforts. V was just recovering from a bad rugby injury to his knee and would find it increasingly difficult sitting for long periods on the hard courtroom benches, so I made him a cushion. I chose beautiful materials - a really heavy yet soft cotton in red, blue, gold, green, black and white. I appliquéd it all together in the Y of the South African flag. The hemming was so perfect I wanted to show it to someone, but there wasn't anyone, and anyway it was a secret - a secret between me and V. I filled it with the softest, most luxurious kapok and embroidered an E in one corner, in red silk. I packed it lovingly in tissue paper and sent it to him by special courier with a note saying, ' *Have Faith, from your friend, E.* '

I actually saw him with it the next day. When we rose for the judge I caught a glimpse of red, green and blue before V sat down again. I had to fight the impulse to raise my fists in victory.

The first time I heard V's voice I was really surprised. It was when the judge asked the defendant to stand. 'Viktor Heiney?, she began, 'You are accused of unlawfully and intentionally killing a person, to whit, Rachel Davey. How do you plead?'

'Not guilty. My Lady.'

A big, strong, rugby star should have a big strong voice shouldn't he? There was a slight tremor when he spoke, as if he was about to burst into tears, so at odds with his good looks and toned body.

That first day he was a fountain of tears. He cried as he made a public apology for what had happened. He was so *very sorry* he sobbed. His girlfriend's death had been a terrible, tragic accident and he was devastated. He cried as he apologised to the Davey family and to Rachel Davey's friends and to his family and supporters. The only person he didn't apologise to was Rachel Davey.

'I woke and saw an intruder coming into the bedroom, my lady, and I panicked. I grabbed my gun and fired. I didn't think. I believed we were being attacked.'

I listened closely to everything V said but what I was really doing was watching him because this was the way I would discover the truth. Surely he could only keep up this facade for so long; eventually there would be a moment - however small - a moment when he gave himself away.

*

Truth to tell I'd been lucky to get into the bail hearing at all on that first day. I was one of the last people allowed in. I'd covered a few cases in this court and when I flashed my shiny Press bracelet at the guy on the door he recognised me and smiled. There were a lot of South African journalists and International journalists covering the trial and the competition for press passes was fierce. I was one of the lucky ones. I'd stolen my bracelet in a press-bar when some stupid cow took it off to wash her hands in the Ladies. I didn't recognise any of our reporters there, which was good for me. *The Chronicle* was a small outfit and the online coverage of the trial would be enough for our columnists.

I was directed to the only space left, directly behind Davey, near the front. I hesitated but the official shrugged and indicated the packed room. Lucky I'm small so I was able to squeeze into the bench beside a large woman. I remembered Terry Davey looking back as I scrambled into my seat, his glance sliding over me and away when he didn't recognise me. His eyes were vacant, like he was drunk or drugged.

The woman beside me refused to shove up so I had to climb over her and her bag and walking stick. She huffed and puffed but eventually I shoe-horned myself into the tiny space between her and another big woman . The heat and sweat radiated off them and that first day was torture. Over time I got used to the discomfort; we all did. The trick was to stay very still.

I had planned to be there early that morning but like all my good intentions it didn't work out. The previous night a few of us from work had gone out for a drink. I was taking a few days off - a sabbatical, someone said. Nice word that, 'sabbatical', gives it a sort of gravitas. They all thought I was going away on holiday - 'somewhere nice.'

'It'll do you good,' one colleague said, 'after...'

'Yep, give you...space to...'

Why did no one finish their sentences around me anymore? Was I that terrifying? I knew the answer to that. Do you ever do that thing when you're walking past a shop window or mirror or something shiny and you suddenly see your face - in repose. I think that's what they call it, like when your expression is really saying what you're feeling, instead of just pretending? Mine must be in repose all the time now. I have to make a conscious effort to unclench my teeth or I get jaw ache.

I drank too much that night and Anton, the smarmy arsehole from Features, took me back to his place. I hope I passed out before anything happened. So, I woke up in a flat on the other side of the city. It was rush hour, I had to get home to change. I hadn't ironed my best shirt. Stupid, stupid. I was worried the hearing might be over by the time I got there. In my experience they only lasted an hour or two - a day at the most and this was an open and shut case. Viktor Heiney had already confessed to killing his girlfriend. All they had to decide was did he get bail and if so, on what terms? In any ordinary case this would have been routine. But this one wasn't 'ordinary.' The accused was a celebrity - a rugby star who played for the Springboks.

*

And surprise, surprise, after several days he did got bail. When it was all over I stayed in my seat while the courtroom cleared. I was in no hurry. V's people gathered around him, smiling, patting his head and shoulders and squeezing his hand - congratulating him. *There, there, little boy, you're safe now.* He had a half smile on his face and there was a flash of his, oh-so-perfect, white teeth.

I was timing my exit. I had remembered to iron my best shirt today and knew I looked good. I wanted to attract V's attention without being obvious. Waiting until he stood up I chose that exact moment to walk quickly along in front of his bench, so that he had to wait while I walked past. I saw he had my cushion under his arm. He looked a bit embarrassed carrying it like that, but it didn't matter because he had my gift and he knew my name. He didn't know me yet but he would.

I turned my head a fraction and gave him my most radiant smile, then walked on quickly, not waiting for a response. One of the things I did well was walking. I was wearing high heels and I knew my legs looked good from the back.

Some guy once said I had beautiful legs, like a young bok's. He was probably taking the piss but I had chosen not to believe that. Funny how some phrases stick in your mind, good and bad. Like my Dad called me a bean-pole once when I was about eleven. I cried all night into my pillow. But sod him, because today I really did look all leggy, like a gazelle.

I could hear them talking animatedly behind me as we walked out and someone laughed. There would be a celebration in the Heiney household that night.

Back Home

After the judge withdrew on that first judgement day I left the courtroom quickly, I needed to get back to the Wendy House to pack. There were crowds of people outside and I had to force my way through. The ANC women's league were keeping vigil, as they had done throughout the trial. Everywhere, there were huge posters of Rachel Davey and other women, unknown women - murdered women.

'Evie? Hello.'

I didn't recognise her at first. She was in a group of traditionally dressed Xhosa women. Her vivid blue turban covered her hair and came down low on her forehead, but as soon as I saw her eyes I knew who it was.

'Mary?' I stepped towards her. 'Is it really you?'

She grasped my hand. 'I have been thinking of you, Evie.'

'You...you okay?'

She nodded. 'You?'

'Fine. Look I'm sorry but I have to go. Things to do, you know?'

'Yes, you are busy doing your job.' She said that with such pride, like I was her favourite child.

I gently took my hand away from hers. 'We must meet up soon, ja?'

'Yes, that would be good.'

She began to say something else but I jumped in. 'Great to see you, Mary,' and turned my back on her, before hurrying away.

15

I didn't stop till I got to the end of the street and looked back over my shoulder. Mary was watching me and smiling. Her hand was half-raised as if she was saying goodbye. I was so ashamed. Mary was as important in our family as any of us and yet I'd no idea how she was managing now we were all gone, or where she was living or anything. But I mustn't think about her now. One day, I promised, one day I'd do something about Mary. Another promise?

After I'd finished packing I returned the key to the landlord. He said he was sorry I was going but we both knew he wasn't. I paid him what I owed, then I caught the train to Stellenbosch. On the train I read Frankie's message again. '...*The Chronicle can't afford an employee who never shows. The proprietors have been very understanding and sympathetic to your situation but that scene in the office was the last straw. Shame, Evie Adze, I had high hopes for you.*'

> *Frankie Vine. Editor. Western Chronicle.*
> '*Come by, and clear your desk.*'

That wouldn't take long. There was nothing in my desk - like my life - except for one thing.

I knew Jane and Dad had put our house on the market but it was still a shock to see the *For Sale* notice . The pole hadn't been put in straight and the wind was rattling the board. I had to push hard to open the gate, forcing my way through a rampant oleander. The once immaculate front garden was a tangle of weeds and trailing plants. Vibrant flowers frantically poked their heads above the green 'water', like drowning swimmers.

I still had my key and let myself in. It was so weird being there again. I stood in the doorway sniffing the air. There were traces of some long ago meal and maybe mice, but the overpowering stink was from those plug-in chemical, air-fresheners. I went around the house pulling them all out of the sockets, then I went into the kitchen and ran the tap until the tepid water ran cooler. I put my face and back of my neck under the running water until my head cleared. Fortunately the electricity was still on - I supposed for prospective buyers - so I filled the kettle and found a jar of coffee and ancient biscuits in the cupboard. I could shop for stuff tomorrow.

Later, I wandered through the rooms. Everything was neat and tidy - no doubt Jane's influence. She'd always been a tidy person. There were one or two pieces of furniture to make it look less bleak when prospective buyers were shown around. Dad's black leather armchair was still there, with a dent in the seat and a slightly dirtier bit of carpet in front of the chair where his feet used to rest. The bedroom that Shon and I had shared had net curtains at the windows. All our old posters had been taken down and the walls painted off-white or whatever fancy-named paint Jane had selected. The whole house was painted the same non-colour. The beds were gone but there were duvets and blankets in the closet and I made a nest on the floor. I lay down fully-dressed. The room

17

had been stripped of everything personal except a frilly bedside light, standing on the floor. I pulled it closer and switched it on. Closing my eyes I thought I might be able to sleep here. This was safe.

When I opened my eyes the following morning the rising sun was incising sharp-edged geometric shapes across the floor. But it wasn't right. The light was coming from the wrong direction and the door wasn't where it should be. I'd been woken by birdsong - the cooing of wood pigeons and the strident call of the hadedah ibis - but there were no hadedahs in my Wendy house garden in Cape Town. It was only when I went to the window and looked out that I remembered where I was. As I was staring out I caught a glimpse of movement at the bottom of the garden. Maybe it was the neighbour's cat or even a dog. Sometimes we got the odd baboon after the bowl of fruit Ma always kept piled high in our kitchen. And that's when a figure came out from behind the vegetation and moved slowly towards the house. Whoever it was, was pushing a wheelbarrow. A gardener? I stood away from the window. I didn't want to be seen.

All the lonely people.

On my way into Cape Town, that morning, the train was full of commuters reading newspapers. Each paper had a similar banner headline, 'Viktor Heiney Guilty?' and beneath there were photos of V and the main protagonists - Thea, Terry Davey, Melanie - these people were my family now - my surrogate, dysfunctional family. I'd been with them throughout the trial.

There was Magda, the wife, who sat in the front bench beside Thea and Davey. Like me, she'd been late for the bail hearing too and had arrived with a man, who sat further back. I never saw her and Davey speak, or even look at each other. She was a smart, rather fierce-looking woman with perfectly straight, black pencilled eyebrows matching her bottle-black hair. She wasn't the mother of Rachel Davey but seemed to enjoy the limelight. The press loved Magda Davey. She liked giving interviews. Three times married, a bit of a hell-raiser in her youth, she was great copy. One day in the courtroom she must have felt me staring at her and flicked a look at me before pressing a handkerchief to her mouth. After all I was press wasn't I?

The other benches on the Davey side were full of friends of the family. Apparently the closest were Oscar and Marisa Needal – the woman read novels during the proceedings while the husband sat with his head bowed. He often fell asleep until she dug him in the ribs and he woke with a snort. Sometimes the whisper of her turning pages and him snoring were the only sounds in the courtroom. There were periods of mind-numbingly boring, nit-

19

picking procedures, then occasional bouts of hyperactivity as the prosecution and defence teams cross-examined witnesses. I think we all envied Oscar Needal and his long sleep.

It was Thea who gave the testimony for Rachel Davey. At the time, her uncle, Terry Davey, was in hospital recovering from a serious chest infection that had led to pneumonia. He missed two weeks of the trial and we thought he'd never come back but one Monday morning, there he was again.

Thea was a small nondescript young woman with short cropped hair, always dressed in trousers and T-shirts. You wouldn't have looked at her twice in a crowd but she gave an impressive speech on behalf of her cousin. She took a deep breath before she started and looked slowly around the courtroom. She wasn't afraid to look people in the eye. When she spoke, her voice was strong.

'Rach and me grew up together. We were like sisters - well more than sisters really, cos there was none of that sibling rivalry you hear about?'

There were some smiles at this.

'After Rach's mum died she spent a lot of time at our house. So did my uncle. We were like one family. Rach was my girls' godmother. They loved their auntie,' her voice broke on those words but she stopped for a moment, then took a deep breath and continued. 'The children, they...they can't sleep. They have nightmares. They're going to trauma therapy - we all are. You see,

I don't know what to tell them… How do you explain something like that to children?'

She hesitated for a moment and I saw her small hands clenching and unclenching.

'We...we're not doing good - the family. We've never been rich but we were close, all of us, we helped each other out if we could. Rach was so generous to us all. But this...this has destroyed us. People have fallen out with each other. The guilt and blame is rotting our relationships, I don't think it will ever be the same again and...' She took a large gulp of air before she spoke again. 'And I... miss her so much.'

She bent her head and we saw her shoulders were shaking. She was crying, but she made no sound. I don't know how she did that. The judge waited for a few moments, then asked her gently if she'd finished. Thea nodded and stumbled back to her seat.

Over the months of the trial I'd followed the gradual decline of Terry Davey. I'd seen his reactions to the bloody evidence, heard every moan, noticed each weary shake of his head. I knew the exact position of the cigarette burns and food stains on his old Safari jacket. I'd watched him morph from an upright, larger than life figure, into this parody of himself. He looked like a stooping, rather creepy Father Christmas, with his longish white, straggly hair and unkempt beard, tinged with dirty yellow.

He wore the same jacket every day and a succession of grubby and grubbier shirts. The collar of his tartan shirt today was frayed and sticking up. I wanted to straighten it for him. He leant forward in his seat, hands clasping the top of the bench in front, his knuckles white from his grim hold. He looked like what he was, an elderly, poor white, and his sadness weighed him down like that albatross around *The Ancient Mariner's* neck. Hard to believe this was the same man who'd once run a fairly successful business and had a home, a wife and a beautiful daughter He'd been hammered by grief into a lesser man.

Just as the old man was shabby and dishevelled, so Viktor Heiney was immaculate and well groomed. His black hair shone, his shoes were highly polished, he wore a dark suit, white shirt and black tie. Maybe his people thought that formal wear showed the young man's remorse. It should have worked but something wasn't quite right. The jacket didn't quite fit, the sleeves were slightly too long and the trousers were roomy, too uncool. They even had a crease in them. He was mid-twenties but he looked like a young boy dressed up in one of his father's cut-downs for the first big social event of his life. So, instead of looking like a well-brought-up, heart-broken penitent, he looked shifty, like a guy dealing dagga in a bar.

Even if you weren't cynical like me, you would have been suspicious of this obvious attempt to airbrush V. Photographs of this rising rugby star were constantly featured on the front pages of magazines. There he'd be, at some trendy night spot, or the first night of a show, accompanied by his beautiful blonde girlfriend,

Rachel Davey. V and Rachel were the new golden couple, the Posh and Becks of the South African celebrity A list. He wore designer jeans, T-shirts and baseball caps. He wouldn't have been seen dead in that suit.

During the never-ending intervals, waiting for something, anything, to happen, I concentrated on V. He had a certain way of sitting when he was relaxed, legs crossed, leaning sideways against the railing, chin resting in his left hand. Then there was the *'I'm paying attention'* position - the ramrod-backed, looking straight-ahead posture with the chin raised. Then the *'oh my God, I can't look'*, with the frantic turning of his head from side to side, as if searching for a way out. And the totally spontaneous tics - the bringing of the index finger up in front of his mouth and tapping it on his lips. The closing of eyes and head tilted back reaching heavenwards. And the tears, the tears. the avalanche of tears.

I'd seen him break down under cross-examination and when describing what had happened the night Rachel Davey was killed. I'd seen him throw up when they'd shown pictures of Rachel Davey's wounds, especially those to her head.

...'please don't make me look again, My Lady. I've seen it all before....I was there. I carried my beautiful girl downstairs. I have blood on my hands...'

You said it Vikky boy.

I'd caught him staring at the attractive female court official sitting in front of him. I'd watched his performance day after day,

23

noting the similarities and the differences. I wanted to Get Inside His Head. V the rugby star, the clean living, god-fearing, truly sorry... 'murderer.' But he'd been cleared of murdering Rachel hadn't he? And he was so very sorry. In the biopic of his trial maybe they'll hire him to play himself. Maybe that would please this 'narcissistic psychopath.' And it wasn't me that had given him that title, every amateur psychiatrist in the world was psycho-analysing him.

His fragile state of mind and obvious grief were key elements in the defence's case. Over and over again we heard psychiatrist and trauma specialist reports on how the accused was suffering from recurring nightmares and PTS. The young man was having therapy and treatment for clinical depression. At this point the prosecution reminded the court that the accused's 9mm hand gun was loaded with 'black talon' ammunition – bullets that opened up into a petal-like shape on impact and were designed for maximum damage. He fired three of these bullets at almost point-blank range into the soft body and head of Rachel Davey...'by mistake'. He must have heard her screams when the first bullet ripped into her - even two neighbours several hundred metres away heard her. Surely V would have recognised the dying screams of the woman he loved? But no, he was in a state of panic and thought it was an intruder; maybe a big black thug with a falsetto voice? And even then, when he must have realised that the 'intruder' had been mortally wounded he shot once more.

In the early days of the trial V threw up into a bucket when Rachel's head injuries were shown - her brain had exploded. After that they kept the bucket in his bench - just in case. He used it again today.

What did we think he was? An animal? He was devastated, he told the court, with real tears running down his face. His life was over. There were a few hollow laughs at this. He was sorry, he said, with such conviction and deep remorse, he said it during bouts of hysteria, he whispered it, he shouted it, he showed it...he really was very, very sorry.

Apparently the Heiney clan was wealthy. They ran several wine estates on the Garden Route. I recognised them from media coverage. There was his uncle, apparently the patriarch of the extensive family, then there was V's sister, Melanie, and his brother, Jan, plus various cousins and relatives. His father had died a few years back and his mother walked out on the family when V was very young. I spotted some faces from the rugby world too and a lot of minor celebs.

Even the people outside in the Square were my 'family'. I'd met several ANC Women's League supporters when I'd been on protest marches with Shon. They were so brave I felt like a fraud when I was with them and kept well away from the police escorts who always trailed them. Some of them must have seen me as I ducked through the crowds but I always looked away. The women's powerful rhythmic singing and chanting formed the backdrop to the unfolding drama in the courtroom. When it was quiet inside, the women's rich voices drifted into that stifling oppressive environment, filling our heads.

There was another group of women too. These were young, mainly white, noisy, blonde, long-legged *kugels*, waving banners, with, *We love Vikky*, and, *V is innocent*, on them. They laughed and shouted, and wore very short summer dresses, their long hair rising and falling in the breeze, as if they were at some beach-party. Newspaper cameramen and television crews dived amongst them like demented mossies. Once or twice I deliberately walked into their shot so I would be seen amongst V's supporters. Anyone who stopped long enough to catch a hack's attention had a microphone stuck in her face. Everyone had an opinion. I ploughed through them all. I have journalists' elbows.

Sentencing - day two

I saw the change in the judge as soon as she entered the courtroom this morning. She had reached a decision. And it wasn't just me who noticed because all over the courtroom people were sitting up straighter, intent on catching every word. Tension prickled like static and I stretched my arms out in front of me holding onto the back of the bench in front, easing my aching shoulders. Even Terry Davey looked at the judge and Magda was alert.

'...The accused made a poor witness. He lost his composure in cross-examination and he seemed more concerned about the impact his answers caused than the questions posed.'

I glanced at V. He was writing furiously then tearing out whole pages from a notepad and passing them forward to his advocates. Thea was saying something to her uncle and he was nodding. The judge cleared her throat and took a sip of water. I stared at her. As usual her face was impassive.

'...It is important that we do not go away from this trial thinking that there is one rule for the rich and famous and another for the poor and disadvantaged..."

Really? So, a black man would have the same treatment as this pampered killer, allowed out on bail to enjoy his celebrity status, to attend training sessions with fellow Springboks? I pressed my fingertips to my forehead, kneading the skin, trying to ease my headache, and in that moment another voice broke into the silence. Terry Davey was shouting something. It was a jumble

27

of words, hate words, profanities, all the syllables and sounds caught in the mesh of a scream. I thanked God I had moved out of that seat.

The woman beside me smiled wryly and whispered. 'You've gotta feel sorry for the poor old guy. Imagine how it feels to lose your daughter like that? Even if she was a slag, she didn't deserve that.'

My fists were clenched. 'Yeah, just imagine.'

I knew exactly how the old man felt. The powerlessness. The fury. He couldn't get at the man who murdered his daughter, or alter the judge's verdict, or kill anyone. His impotence was burning him up and I knew that rage.

Davey was shaking violently. I thought he might be having a fit. Thea pulled him into her arms as if he was her baby, soothing him, murmuring to him and gradually he quietened. The judge called up the defence and prosecuting councils. I hoped the old man wasn't going to be thrown out. That would have been too cruel. But the judge waited for several agonising minutes and then continued. She was compassionate, if nothing else.

' Society cannot always get what it wants. Courts exist to dispense justice...'

V was staring intently at the judge. Melanie was sobbing and the uncle had his arms around her. All that angst and none of it mattered, not really, whatever the outcome. You see, it had always been about him and me, forget the rest. All the evidence, the 109

28

witnesses, all the talking, the sheer farce and horror on a daily basis and the words, the endless meaningless words.

'The general public may not even know the difference between punishment and vengeance...'

Vengeance? Davey swore out loud. He was moving around in his seat again, agitated and muttering. Thea looked despairingly about her for help but there was no one. Even Magda had moved away to the end of the bench, distancing herself from the man who used to be her husband.

'...the victim was young, vivacious, full of life...a promising young woman who cared deeply for her family and was full of hope for the future and lived life to the full. '

Do you remember the Miss World contests? Shon and I used to watch repeats when we were kids. They made us laugh, and sometimes we'd put on our swimmers and prance about in Ma's high heels, wiggling our non-existent hips. We especially liked the bit when the beauty queen was interviewed in her sash and the smirking compere asked what they wanted to do with their lives. We learnt their answers by heart and used to chant in unison as we teetered around our living room.' *I want to live life to the full. And work with disadvantaged children, or the disabled, or old people or the drunk and disorderly, or the fat people.* ' The list got longer and longer every time, as we thought up more and more silly things.

But this was no stupid game-show. This was a court of law and a high court judge was talking about a young woman who'd been butchered by her lover. So? If the victim' hadn't been young, beautiful and loved her Dad, wouldn't we care so much? Even in the most brutal of murders does it make it worse if the victim's hot?

For weeks the papers had been full of the possible outcome of this trial. The bookmakers' odds were high for culpable homicide. This sentence carried a five to ten year term with possible parole after 10 months and house arrest for the remainder of the sentence. The alternative fifteen to twenty year custodial sentence had much longer odds. For this judgement the prosecution had to prove beyond reasonable doubt that there was enough circumstantial evidence to prove that the killing was premeditated.

When the judge finished her preliminary summing up she requested that the video footage of Rachel Davey's injuries be shown one last time. I've no idea why she did this. A court official gave the usual warning about the disturbing nature of the material and the screens were turned on. Up till then Davey and Thea had never watched the videos. I'd seen them afterwards on YouTube. Thea always covered her face with her hands and the old man sat, head bowed, with his eyes screwed tight shut. He never opened them again until they were all done.

I saw one of the prosecution lawyers lean back and whisper urgently to them. I was too far away to hear but I knew what he said...'Look away now.' But this time Terry Davey didn't look

30

away. He got slowly to his feet and faced the screens. Thea stood beside him, holding his hand.

I'd watched it so many times I thought I was immune. It was a kid's cartoon, a Tom & Jerry or Bugs Bunny, where no one ever got hurt however many times they fell off a cliff or got blown up. There was no blood in those cartoons. But today I saw the images through the old man's eyes. Saw his body jerk as each bullet entered his daughter's soft skin and skull.

At first the shots were jumbled, vague shapes that slowly unravelled across the screens, then the amorphous mess cleared and there was a face, some sort of a face...yes...two eyes, no, one eye and something like a nose and half a mouth - a lopsided, pretty mouth and blood and bone and teeth and... I began to sweat and my mouth was watering. Leaning forwards I rested my head in my lap. I mustn't be sick. Please, God, don't let me spew up. I took deep breaths and finally the nausea drifted away.

When the screens went blank the Judge asked V to stand.

He got unsteadily to his feet and faced her. He was sobbing uncontrollably.

'It is the unanimous judgement of this court that the accused, Viktor Heiney, will serve five years for culpable homicide and negligent killing, in the shooting to death of the victim.'

There was complete silence. No one moved. There were no expletives or spontaneous shouts of joy – nothing, just the shuffling of papers as the legal teams packed away their words.

31

The judge looked at Terry Davey, who was still standing. 'Hopefully this sentence shall provide some sort of closure to the family so they can move on with their lives.'

Davey didn't hear her, he was staring at the screens. I'm not sure he'd heard the verdict. Thea touched his arm and he flinched as if she'd hurt him. He seemed disorientated but then he slowly turned to face the public. He had a sort of smile on his face, a dead man's smile, and one of his hands flapped against his leg like a dying fish.

But then he seemed to draw some strength from somewhere and he drew himself up in a semblance of what the old Terry Davey must have looked like. His voice was loud and clear. 'She's not *'the girlfriend,'* or *'the model'*, or *'the deceased,'* or *'the victim'* or *'the twenty-year-old student'*. She's got a name. My daughter's got a name. Rachel Davey. Remember that. Always remember that. She was murdered in cold blood by that ...thing... And he's got away with it. They say ten months in prison. Ten months for murdering my beautiful daughter. A boy got put away for a year for shooting a dog. My girl, she's not even as important as a dog.'

Thea jumped up beside her uncle. 'Shame on you,' she shouted at the top of her voice. 'Shame on you, shame on us all.'

Davey and Thea were hustled out of the courtroom but we could still hear him shouting, long after the big heavy doors banged shut behind them.

'Whichever stone you crawl under, I'll find you, Heiney. There's nowhere to go. You're dead!' 'And then another door slammed further away and there was silence.

The girl in front of V ran her fingers through her hair and patted it into place. I saw him glance up at her and I felt rage pumping through me. I remembered another man, another bastard murderer.

We waited until the judge hurried out of the court and V was taken down to the cells. No one moved until someone coughed and that seemed to be the signal for everyone to collect their belongings together and leave. But even as people got to their feet, stretching and murmuring to each other, even as they made their way to the exit, the words were still running into each other in my brain like some sort of tantric chant. *He was really very, very, very sorry.* Maybe, if I keep hearing them, they'll be true.

I knew the power of words and language, especially the legal juggernaut of language. My father was a lawyer, he used words to get his way, at home, at work, in his mind. He was a king of words, an emperor, and he wielded that power like a despot. They all do. Especially the words that keep a lesser breed to heel. Why are we impressed by these ponderous legal phrases? Do they make us believe that justice has been done?

But, even after all these words, what was clear was that Terry Davey was right, a woman's life was worth less than a dog's. Yes, V shot Rachel Davey but...but he thought she was an intruder, a nightmare black man with rape and murder on his tik-filled, psychotic brain. The huge black man was going to knock V out, tie him up, then make him watch while he screwed the woman he loved until she died. So? what else could he do? He shot the intruder, not once, not twice but three times with a heavy calibre handgun. Wouldn't you have done the same?

Dan Kinelly

I met Dan Kinelly in the flat time between V's conviction and the judge's sentencing - it was about six months in total. I was working then, keeping my head down, surviving.

Dan arrived one morning straight off the plane from the UK, carrying a small backpack and his laptop. It was very hot, even by Cape Town standards, and he was wearing UK winter clothes. He had sandy hair and pale skin and his face was brick red. He managed a grin as the sweat dripped off the end of his nose. 'Water, water,' he croaked, and pretended to collapse on the floor. Someone chucked him a T-shirt with *Western Chronicle* plastered across the front. A stack of shirts had been donated to the paper by a grateful client after a successful advertising campaign for their wors. On the back of the shirt was a huge link of prime boerewors, with the slogan. *Get your lips around that.* We all refused to wear them but Dan took the lot and wore a different one every day.

He was on a two-year secondment from the newspaper he worked on in Belfast and was renting a room with a contact from his paper. Dan was a freelance as well as a journalist and was writing a book about Mandela. When someone asked why, when there were hundreds of books about the great man already, Dan Kinelly winked and tapped the side of his nose.

'None of them will be as good as mine. You'll have heard of Brendan Behan? Well, I'm the half-blood of his second cousin, twice removed, on my grandmother's side.'

A gang of us from work used to go out on Friday nights for a drink and Dan soon became one of the regulars. He was really into World music and Abdullah Ibrahim (aka Dollar Brand) was a hero of his. It was coming up to the Mardi Gras and the harbour-side bars and cafes were full of Cape jazz musicians strutting their stuff. I remember Dan so well from back then. He was a typical Irishman and could always find something to say but once the music started he was totally lost. No one could get a word out of him. I loved jazz too, especially the famous Cape Jazz Band (CJB). Once upon a time I had their *Musical Democracy* on a loop in my car. Dan and I used to argue about who were the best bands.

He seemed nice, friendly but not pushy - unlike most of the other guys, who weren't interested in you unless you had sex with them. The whole *Lad* culture thing made me sick but I went along with it because I didn't care what happened to me, or what anyone thought about me.

I was living just around the corner from Dan so we sometimes bumped into each other. He was funny and relaxed and talked non-stop, which was lucky because I didn't have a lot to say. One night before we went our separate ways he asked me what I thought of him. Typical that. He liked to put people on the spot, so I told him he was my idea of a typical Paddy - full of bull-shit. He laughed and then he gave me a long look and I thought, *Uh, uh, here it comes. He's gonna hit on me.* He must have heard about my reputation by now. *Evie Adze is easy.* Thing was I liked him but I didn't want any complications in my life. He was still staring so I asked him straight out what the problem was. He blushed. He actually blushed.

'Sorry,' he smiled. 'I didn't mean to stare but I'm just wondering who you are, Evie Adze.'

That's what he said. Not how gorgeous I was, or how he fancied me, or anything crass.

'I mean, you don't talk about yourself - ever. I don't know how you tick. You're an enigma,' he finished lamely.

'You want to know who I am?'

He nodded.

'I'm no-one, Dan.' I said, trying to make it sound like a joke. 'That's all you need to know.'

'Perfect combo then,' he said, grinning. 'You're *no-one* and I'm *the professional Paddy*. Two great disguises.'

Soon after this we got to travelling to work together. I had a bike and I borrowed one off my landlord for Dan. I taught him the rudiments of survival in Cape Town traffic, like how to deal with four-way stops and how to beat the rush-hour mayhem by riding on the pavements. At weekends we explored the city. Dan wanted to know everything about Cape Town. He was especially interested in District Six - the Creole working-class township on the Cape Flats - where a lot of the great jazz came from. His enthusiasm was catching and it was great seeing my city through his eyes. Shon and I loved coming to the city when we were teenagers. We did a lot of growing up in Cape Town.

For the first time in over a year I had something to get up for in the mornings. I knew it was only temporary but it felt good.

Dan was a crap cyclist, so I was totally surprised when he bounced into the newsroom one morning and tossed a tourist-flyer down in front of me. *'Table Mountain, Double Descent. Do it by bike and see the wonderful panoramic views of where the mighty Atlantic meets the exotic Indian Ocean.'*

'What d'you reckon? Are you up for it?'

'Er...' I hesitated, trying to think of a polite way to say *no*.

'Aren't you interested?'

'Sounds good but...'

'...You've done it before?'

I shook my head. 'No, but it's not really my thing.'

'What isn't? Having fun?'

I shrugged.

'Come on, Evie. I might never get the chance to see where *'the mighty Atlantic meets the exotic Indian Ocean,'* again. The Irish Sea doesn't have quite the same allure does it? Please. I need a back-up team in case I collapse.'

'If I'm absolutely honest, Dan, I'm not sure you're quite ready for something like this.' I saw his expression. I should have known better than to question a man's machismo. I hurried on, 'All I'm saying is, it's not easy.'

'No pain, no gain. Anyway,' he said, jabbing his finger at the flyer. ' Kids do it. Look, See that boy? Can't be more than, what, ten?'

So, that's how we came to be halfway up Table Mountain in a cable-car plus our rented mountain bikes, with their front suspension and hydraulic disc brakes. We were part of a larger group with a guide and teenagers, who whooped and hollered all the way to the top. We would be riding down the South side of the mountain on mainly off-road dirt tracks and private roads and then along the front of the mountain, taking in Devil's Peak. Dan was unusually quiet on the way to the top and even quieter when we got out and he looked over the edge. Panic didn't begin to cover the expression on his face as he watched our cosy gondola swing away from us and disappear. He stared at me, his mouth opening and closing.

The guide chose that moment to smack him on the back and yell. 'Okay guys. It's all downhill from here. The slower you go the easier it is, the faster you go the more exciting it gets.' And with that, he leapt on his bike and disappeared over the edge. All the other eager bikers followed him. We could hear their *Geronimos* and *Yeehas* for a long time after they'd disappeared.'

'It'll be okay, Dan. We'll take it easy.' I pedalled to the top of the track and waited, but Dan's bike wasn't moving at all. 'Ease off the brake a bit, Dan.' Inch by inch he came towards me until we gently dropped down onto the track. I could see the sweat running down his neck. 'You got lots of sun screen on? Dan?' But he wasn't listening. I led the way, going as slowly as I could on that precipitous gradient. I could hear his heavy breathing behind me and there weren't any *yeehas*. We couldn't have stopped, even if we wanted to, because there was a sheer drop on one side and a towering rock face on the other.

Several years later, when we finally caught up with the others, they cheered and immediately leapt on their bikes and pedalled furiously away. Dan fell off his bike and sank down onto the ground, burying his head in his hands and moaning gently.

When he could speak, his voice had gone up several octaves. 'My heart's pumping so fast it feels like a jack hammer in my chest and look at my hands, Evie. Is that normal?' His hands were jerking uncontrollably. 'That was the most terrifying thing I have ever done in my life, bar none - switch-back bends and sheer drops. They didn't mention that in the brochure.' Eventually he managed to crawl onto his knees and then he pointed a shaking finger up at the grinning mountain. 'Race you to the top.'

Bit by bit, smile by smile, the ice around my heart was melting. Maybe...just maybe...

A few days after the bike ride Dan asked me to go for a meal with him. I didn't want to but he kept on and on at me until I said *yes*. We trawled the length of Long Street - the trendiest area in Cape Town - and ended up in a small bistro down a side street, eating

Cape Malay food and listening to one guy playing sweet jazz on a sax.

I liked being with him. There was something really liberating about us having no shared history, either personal or emotional. He didn't talk about himself or his family or anything from his life in Ireland. He lived in the present and I liked that. Of course, he must have known about Shon but he didn't ask any awkward questions or say he was sorry. He wasn't tiptoeing around me like everyone else. I'm not saying he made me forget what had happened, no one could do that, but it was good to relax a bit.

He was so kind that night and whatever happened at the end of it, he'd earned it. He held the door open for me, took my elbow crossing the road, asked more than once if I was too warm, too cold, hungry? 'No, not hungry,' I remember laughing. 'But I wouldn't say no to a drink or ten.' And I regretted it as soon as the stupid words were out of my big gob. And for the first time in a long time I thought that perhaps I might stop before I got drunk, just this once. I knew the booze was getting to me. The irony is that I'd never liked the taste of alcohol. I used it as an anaesthetic.

After the meal we ambled down to the waterfront and stood, side by side, watching the sea washing in against the harbour walls and the lights falling on the water, like slicks of bright paint.

'God, Evie. Do you know how lucky you are living in a place like this? It's just gorgeous.'

41

'What? Even with all our problems?'

'Every country has its problems. Look at Ireland. And we've got a helluva lot of rain too.'

'We get rain.'

'Yeah, but then *the sun comes out and dries up all the rain, And incy-wincy spider climbs up the spout again.*

He took my hand as we strolled back home. His grasp was firm and I felt like a child again. It was like he was my protector. Stupid. We were silent as we walked. I was worrying about what happened next. It wasn't that I didn't fancy him, but I couldn't invite him back to my place and...he hadn't mentioned his. I needn't have worried though because he led me to my little front door, took the key, unlocked the door and switched the lights on, as if he knew I was scared of the dark. Then he gave me a hug and disappeared into the night. 'See you in the morning, Evie Adze.'

In those few months with Dan I felt almost normal. We had so much in common. We relished debunking pretentious people and you get a lot of those in the newspaper world. Dan could spot a phoney a mile off. Another great thing was that we worked well together. He arrived just after Mandela died and Frankie assigned us to a series of articles on 'Madiba's' last days, plus the pros and cons of the Mandela family feud. Frankie thought it would be good to get an insider's and outsider's take on the great man's legacy. We made a good team. Dan was the professional Irishman with the twinkly smile and the red hair, and I was the hard as nails, intrusive hack. I asked the nasty questions and he sugared them with a joke or a laugh.

He was a compulsive scribbler and never went anywhere without his little note-book and backpack stuffed with research information. He was cagey about the book he was working on but I knew lots of writers like that. A prestigious UK publishing house had already paid a hefty advance on the book. I was glad for him but also envious. He was so driven. My novel and all the different beginnings were gathering dust on my laptop. I'll never finish it now.

We still hadn't slept together but that wasn't a problem for me. Dan seemed okay about it too. It wasn't just me who liked him and I'm sure there were plenty of women willing to jump into bed with him. I'd never had a male friend before and it felt good. There was none of that flirting and getting dressed up and worrying about your hair or your boobs or whatever. If I looked shit he told me and vice versa. He said once that I'd looked like some poor wretch out of Belsen when he first arrived, and saw it as a challenge to fatten me up.

Growing up with sisters and going to an all-girls school I hadn't had much experience with men. I don't think my Dad was much of a male role model either. Dan was like my best mate. I don't know whether he had a wife or girlfriend at home, I somehow didn't think so, but it didn't matter. I would have told Dan anything, if he'd asked. You see, I trusted him.

Treachery

Dan got on well with everybody, including my landlord. So he often dropped by my place after work with a bottle of wine. We spent a lot of time in the little garden outside my Wendy house. It was shaded and cool on summer evenings.

On the night it happened we were on the stoep watching the sun go down over Table Mountain. The mountain's white *table cloth* was spectacular in the dying light.

'I can see why people call Cape Town 'Mother'. ' Dan said, suddenly, rolling his wine around the glass and watching the liquid change colour in the dying light. 'The mountains on one side and the sea on the other, it's like we're being held in the city's gentle caress, like a tiny baby. '

'Where did that come from?' I asked.

'Dunno,' Dan had come round to show me his latest South African acquisition. He'd need a very large case to take all his stuff back to the UK. This time he'd bought a Ghomma, a wooden, barrel-shaped Asian-type drum, used in Goema jazz - another form of Cape jazz. I was never keen on loud drumming, but this one made a pleasant, almost melodic sound, and Dan was loving it. He had such a great smile when he was totally engrossed in something, like he was in love with it.

It should have been an idyllic night but I was nervous and I knew he'd picked up on my mood.

He stopped playing and took a drink of his wine. 'Everything okay, Evie?'

'Yeah, fine.' But it wasn't. I was building up to telling him that I wouldn't be coming into work for a few days. V's sentencing was scheduled for the following Monday. Soon it would all be over and then what?

I went back inside to get more chips and Dan followed. I gave him the dish, expecting him to go back outside. I'd made rum truffles and they were cooling on a tray. There were twelve. I always made twelve. Ten to a box and two spare, in case of accidents.

Dan leant over and popped one in his mouth. 'Yum, didn't know you made these. My absolute top favourites, after liquorice allsorts and black bullets.'

'Black bullets?' I said, trying to distract him.

'Honest to God, they're fantastic, aniseedy, sweet, break your teeth if you bite into them.'

While he chattered I put the tray out of his reach.

'One more. Go on Evie, there are loads.'

'No, I need ten, each box has ten...

'God, you're pernickety.'

'Pernickety? What sort of a word is that?'

'Perfectly ordinary word, Evie. Anyway why the truffles?'

'They're a present.'

'Really? Who for?'

I shrugged. I was smiling but I knew my hands were trembling. He must have noticed because he went outside again without a word. I packed up ten perfect truffles in their little gold

45

cases with red tissue paper and slipped it inside a padded envelope, ready for posting. The eleventh truffle went in the bin. I always threw the extras away. I hated truffles.

Dan was scribbling in his notebook when I went out so I started on the flower beds. Gardening always relaxed me. I was dividing and transplanting clivias and agapanthus. The clivias were the delicate pale yellow variety, not so garish as the more common bright orange ones. I hadn't felt like gardening for such a long time. Originally it had been part of the deal for my living cheaply in this annexe. Love of gardening had been something that Ma had passed on to me. It was probably the one thing we shared. She should have been a botanist like her dad but she said nursing was a bit like gardening. You found out what the plant was lacking and gave them the appropriate 'medicine'. Our garden at home was the best in the street. Ma loved all plants, be they common, exotic, medicinal, aliens, or the gorgeous indigenous fynbos plants. She still had relations in the UK who sent out bulbs and we had the most amazing spring garden. People used to come and hang over our fence just to admire it. She opened it once a year for a local children's charity.

Sitting back on my heels I stretched my arms above my head. I would be stiff tomorrow. I can't explain how good it was to have dirt under my fingernails again and to smell the warm musky earth. Ma always said that the spring soil smelt differently from the rest of the year. 'It's the terpenes,' she said, whatever they were.

46

It was the smell of new growth, where anything was possible, and some plant you'd been trying to grow for years might just blossom this time. There was always hope.

She also taught me about the toxicity of plants. *'Treat every plant with respect,'* she'd say *'and never eat anything you're not sure of. Understand?'* We had the most beautiful little shrubby tree in our garden, an acokanthera oppositifolia. Ma taught me all the Latin names. I used to love the feel of those words in my mouth. It was a secret language between her and me. It made me feel special. Sometimes I chanted the words over and over again like a mantra until Shon threw something at me. Anyway, this particular tree was a little gem. It had pretty perfumed white flowers tinged with pink and delicious looking purple fruits that we knew we mustn't eat. The plant was incredibly toxic and I remember Dad getting really upset about it.

'You should take that out and burn it.'

But Ma just smiled and said, 'They know it's poisonous. I've warned them enough times.'

'So? Is this another example of your famous child rearing techniques? They only learn from their mistakes? But in this case they wouldn't learn because they'd be dead. You know how it works don't you?'

'Of course. I'm a nurse for God's sake. The toxins paralyze the respiratory system, resulting in asphyxiation.'

'And then they die?'

'Yes, but it's only the bark and stems of the tree that are really lethal.'

'Oh, that's all right then.'

She'd laughed and kissed his cheek but he wouldn't be distracted. 'Why d'you think they call it *Bushman's Poison* for God's sake?'

'It's also called *Wintersweet* too because it's a remedy for snakebites, rashes, worms and is excellent for...'

'...Poison arrows?'

They both laughed at that. I'd forgotten how they sometimes did that - laughed together.

The little tree stayed where it was throughout our childhood. Ma taught us that every garden was full of poisonous plants and occasional scorpions. It's not nice to be zapped by a scorpion. I sat on a little one once. The little ones are often the most painful. My bum swelled up like a football. There were also spiders and snakes. We were particularly careful if we went in the garden at night. Puff adders liked to lie about in the dark, pretending to be pieces of wood, so they could catch tasty rodents, like the pretty little mice with red stripes down their backs.

I stood up and took the tools back to the shed. Dan was still writing when I got back and I held up the bottle of wine.

'Umm,' he muttered, holding out his glass. He was totally absorbed in what he was doing and I watched as he wrote. He was left handed and it always fascinated me how he held his pen and

48

the pad. It looked so awkward. He had nice hands, long fingers, almost artistic. I studied his face. He wasn't good looking in the accepted sense but there was something about him. His head was a lovely shape, perfectly proportioned and his hair was thick and glossy. He had this habit of running his fingers through it when he was concentrating, like now, so that it stuck up like a little boy's. He must have sensed me looking at him because he put down his pen and shut his notebook. 'So? What's on your mind, Evie?'

'Nothing. Just thinking.' I flushed, feeling as if I'd been caught doing something wrong.

'You seem a bit...twitchy tonight?'

'I'm fine.' I flopped down into my chair and had a drink of wine. I must have sounded more annoyed than I felt because he gave me a *what's wrong with you* look. I tried to keep my tone light. 'Umm, nice. Where d'you get it?'

'Spar, cheap as chips.'

I smiled. 'Chips? Now would that be crisps or slap chips?'

'Whatever's the cheapest.'

We both took another sip of wine.

It was now or never. 'Don't know whether I told you, Dan, but I'm off work for a few days, starting this Friday.'

He stared at me over the rim of his glass, then he clinked his glass against mine, 'Cool. Going somewhere nice?'

'Not really.'

' Something cropped up?'

'No, I just felt like a break. There's no law against that, is there?'

'Nope.'

'I just wanted to get away for a bit.'

'Going with friends?'

'What is this, the third degree?'

He hitched his chair closer and rested his hand on mine. 'And you're sure there's nothing you want to tell me?'

'No. How many times, for God's sake.' I pulled my hand free. 'So? My turn. I want to know what you're writing in that book of yours?'

He raised his eyebrows and said in his best Noel Coward voice. 'Darling. One should always keep a notebook to record anything that one thinks might be useful in one's writing. Snippets of conversation and bonmots from newspapers or quotes from famous people and so on.'

'And your life?'

He made a face, 'Na, that's boring.'

I laughed and held out my hand, 'Okay, I'll just have to see for myself then.'

He flipped through some pages and showed me some intricate detailed doodlings and thumbnail caricatures of people in the office. Frankie's was great. He was really very good. 'I didn't know you were an artist too. Let's see some more.'

He was still smiling but he shook his head. 'No, sorry Evie. It's…it's private.'

50

'Ah ha,' I laughed. 'So, my little Irish leprechaun has got some skeletons in the cupboard?' and I snatched the book off him and flicked it open.

'Give that back, now,' he roared, grabbing my arm and trying to get at the book.

I thought he was joking and I turned my back on him, holding the book above my head. He spun me around, trying to wrestle it out of my hands but I was still hanging on. That's when I caught a glimpse of his face. He was panting and wild-eyed and I thought he was going to hit me. I shrank back and the book fell at our feet. The pages fanned out and papers and cuttings flew everywhere. He dropped to his knees, frantically shovelling them into his backpack. I got down beside him to help but he pushed me roughly aside. I had a handful of cuttings and I held them out to him. 'I'm sorry, Dan I didn't mean...', but then I saw what I was holding.

The headlines ran, *'Cape Town actor murders model girlfriend in Tik-fuelled frenzy.'* *'Nick Ground flees South Africa.'* *'Interpol's failure to apprehend Nick Ground.'* Then there was a picture of Shon in a skimpy bikini, smiling and beautiful with Nick Ground standing beside her, one arm around her waist and the other hand clasped possessively around her brown arm. He was making a funny face at her and she was sticking out her tongue. I let the news-cuttings slip through my fingers and then they fluttered across the table and out into the street.

I turned away from Dan and he put his hand on my shoulder. 'I'm so sorry, Evie. It's not what you think, please let me explain.'

I jammed my elbows backwards into his ribs and I heard him grunt with pain. 'I thought you were my friend,' I shrieked, 'and all the time you were using me. Get out. Go on. Get out of here.'

I wanted to call in sick the next day but I had to hand over the finished article to Frankie. I owed her that. It was still early when I got there and I was hurrying to print the copy off when Dan arrived. He breezed into the office as if nothing had happened and perched on my desk. He was carrying two coffees and he put one down in front of me.

'Mornin', Evie. I texted but you weren't picking up. God! the traffic this morning was diabolical. Your bike wasn't here, are you parking somewhere else?'

I kept my eyes on the screen, waiting for him to go.

'Are you going to let me explain?'

I was silent.

'Okay, I get it, Kinelly boobed. You're right, I should have told you what I was doing. Good for you. You're gonna make me suffer. It was nothing, I promise - those cuttings - I told you I'm obsessive. I hoard everything I'm interested in. Force of habit.'

He waited for me to speak but I didn't. I knew the power of silence.

'Please, say something.'

I stopped typing and looked him straight in the eye. 'Are you writing a book about ...about my sister?'

'No, of course not.' he looked away, 'well...not specifically, I'm doing a piece on domestic violence in South Africa. I know that your sister was very involved in the anti-rape movement.' He waited for me to say something but I didn't. 'It's just a small part of my book - a chapter or two. The case was a remarkable one, Evie...Sorry that's the wrong word. It must have been...I can't imagine how awful it must have been.'

'You were using me.'

'No. Of course not. I wouldn't do that. We're friends.'

I stood up and went to the printer and he followed. As I waited for the document to come through he touched my arm and leant towards me as if he was going to hug me. I stepped away from him. My fists were clenched 'Just get out of my life. I don't need you, I don't need anyone. Now piss off!'

'You don't mean that.'

'I do. I never want to see you again,' I swept up the printed document and marched back to my desk.

He stood for a moment staring at me as if he couldn't quite believe what had happened, then he grabbed his coffee and walked quickly away.

'And take this with you,' I yelled, hurling the other cup after him. It hit him squarely on the back and the lid flipped off and hot coffee arced up and over him. It must have burnt because he raced for the loo. Did I actually do that? Was that me? There was a spreading pool of liquid on the floor and several people were frantically mopping coffee off their computers and files. Someone shouted, 'Shit. What's that crazy bitch done now?'

When I dared to look, they all had their heads down pretending to work. I picked up my bag and fled. I didn't stop running till I reached the end of the street.

After

After the sentencing I came out into the bright, clear light of an early summer's day. Surely this wasn't it? There must be more? I wasn't ready for what happened next. My heart was thudding.

There were people all around me, jostling, pushing, laughing, crying, but I felt so alone. It was like I was the last person on the earth and night was falling.

Mary was there. She was in a group of women standing in a circle, facing each other, not touching, totally still. At least that's what I thought but then I saw that they were swaying backwards and forwards, gently rocking, keeping their heads bowed.

I hunched down but Mary wasn't looking at me, or anyone. Her tears were blinding her. And suddenly I remembered a day, the day I last saw Mary cry. I'd run in from school and the house was full of the smell of baking, so I crashed into the kitchen, demanding rusks and juice. Ma and Mary were sitting at the kitchen table. Ma looked up at me and put her finger to her lips. I'd never seen my mother look so sad. I was a child but I knew I mustn't disturb them and I tiptoed away. After that Mary lived in the little shed at the bottom of our garden. No one ever said why but we knew it was something bad. Where was she sleeping now? Too late to show concern - much too late.

I stumbled on past the groups of black and coloured women. Most of them looked stunned. If this was judgement for a murdered white girl what hope was there for them? What hope was there for the brave women in the police stations reporting rape, only to be raped again by the police? What hope for any woman?

The Women's League supporters were packing up their tents and heading home. They were loud and belligerent in their disgust at the lenient sentence, but they were used to disappointment. One of their placards lay abandoned in the dirt, while people trampled it into the dust. *Justice for black women too.* I heard Shon's voice then, so clearly, I almost expected to see her standing there beside me. I walked quickly away not looking where I was going and barged into a young woman.

'Ag, that was my foot.'

The girl and her friend were dressed in identical tight, black shorts and T-shirts with *Vikky* in red sparkly letters printed across the front. They must have seen my reaction because the one I'd walked into made a face and said something under her breath and they both laughed. I pushed between them and hurried away. I could still hear their laughter. All I wanted was to get away from that place but there were crowds everywhere, milling about, many of them looking as shell-shocked as me. I needed to find somewhere quiet to wait until the crowd thinned and I could make a run for it.

Turning right I headed down a street lined with coral trees. The red of the blossom blazed out at me and I put on my sunglasses. They protected my eyes from the glare and hid my tears. I hadn't meant to cry. I wanted to stay angry. But after the emotion and horror of that claustrophobic courtroom, the vibrancy

56

and beauty of that day felt like vomit in the back of my throat. I saw several people I knew, including the woman reporter I'd sat beside. She was pushing her way through the crowd towards me, so I ducked into a cafe and ordered something. The only space left was a seat beside the two women I'd bumped into outside. They glanced at me and moved closer together; their long blond hair spilled across their faces as they whispered and giggled to each other.

I felt calmer away from the frenetic crowds and took out my cell. I tweeted Melanie. *'Justice has been done. Thank God. In a few months time Viktor will be home with his loved ones. All love E.'*

The Courthouse exit was opposite where I was sitting and I watched as television crews and reporters crowded the base of the steps leading up to the huge doors. Police had formed a cordon down either side of the steps. I needn't have worried about being recognised because, at that moment, there was a buzz of excitement as the old man emerged into the sunshine. He was flanked by his supporters and clutching Thea's hand. All eyes and lenses were on him.

Only yesterday the media circus had been staking out the back of the building, hoping to get a shot of V. *'The rise and fall of a global icon.'* This was the same man who had visited Nelson Mandela just before he died. They had liked each other, according to the tabloids. V was a clean-living, God-fearing man who supported his family, did charity work for underprivileged kids.

God bless him, he'd even set up a rugby academy in the Cape Flats. But today everything had changed. There was fresh blood. Here was something truly newsworthy. Who cared that a man had got away with murdering a woman in South Africa? Where was the hook in that? What do the stats say? A woman killed in domestic violence every eight hours - the vast majority black or mixed race – so mostly reported, if at all, in small print somewhere in the middle of the newspaper. Up to now this gruesome murder had made good copy, it ticked all the boxes - high profile glamorous couple and bloody murder with added titillation and possible sexual perversion. The editors must have been wetting themselves, but that was then and now there was a deranged, dangerous old man, swearing to kill the celebrity killer of his daughter. No contest.

Davey hesitated on the top step and looked down at the waiting paparazzi, the whole clicking, flashing, screaming scrum of them. *Look this way, Mr Davey. What d'you think of the sentence, Mr Davey? Are you going to appeal?*

Davey raised his head and bellowed at the baying crowd. 'Did you see her? Did you? That was her, that was my lovely...my lovely, sweet baby.' His tears and snot ran together down his cheeks and he swiped at them angrily with the back of his sleeve. He pointed a shaking finger at the people. 'Don't have kids.' He was crying now, great gouts of grief. 'Don't ever have kids - especially a girl. They said she was a slag, slept around. All those lies about her. Opening her legs for anyone. But it's not true. She was a good girl, her mum saw to that, she was a good girl. Tell them, tell everyone.'

And at last, he was done, all the fight went out of him and Thea took his hand. There was only one way down and his people pressed forward.

The women beside me were watching him too and sniggering. 'To Viktor', one of them said, clinking her glass against her friend's.

Leaning towards them I smiled. 'Viktor Heiney is going to die.' They turned their shocked little faces to me and I laughed. 'Ah, shame, didn't you know? ' Then I took their bottle and drank from it. 'Cheers,' I said, wine spilling down my neck and soaking my top. For a moment they stared at me like terrified animals trapped in a car's headlights, then they grabbed their handbags and ran. I wasn't frightened anymore because it was so simple. I knew I could do it.

Terry Davey stared vacantly around, then he squeezed his eyes tight shut and began the descent. Thea held his arm tightly helping him down each step. He was muttering to himself. Every stride he took was a tragedy waiting to happen, only diverted by that strong young woman at his side. They were trailed by the weeping Magda, then came the Needals, close behind. There was an argument going on between the two women as they jockeyed for pole position behind Davey. Marisa Needal was attempting to push Magda aside so that she and the still sleepy Oscar could be the train-bearers. I'd read somewhere that there was no love lost between these people. But the grief-stricken Magda was not going to be ousted – this was her moment. After all she was still Davey's wife and had priority. If things went well she might even move back in with him, *to care for her grief stricken husband*, as she put it in the Sunday glossies. *I know where my duty lies*. But the Needals, especially Marisa, had been friends with Terry *and his darling wife, who died so tragically when Rachel was a tot,* had always been close to Terry, *'apart from that period when he had the most inappropriate young girlfriend and went off the rails.* That was all in the papers too, every bit of dirt, real or imaginary. One rag hinted that Terry Davey had been lonely when his wife died and his little daughter was very pretty and very loving. They didn't actually spell it out but the seed had been sown. And now, of course, there was Thea. She must be gay because she had short hair.

The women were neck and neck now, pushing and shoving like old tortoises, their wrinkled necks sticking out as far as they could go. Then, Oscar Needal got involved and tried to pull his wife away, justifiably embarrassed by the unseemly behaviour of the women, but all he succeeded in doing was unbalancing them. Someone's heel got caught in a flowing skirt and the whole cohort of crazies collapsed down the marble steps knocking aside Thea and crashing into the old man's back. There was nothing anyone could do but watch in horror as the old man was thrown forward into thin air, arms outstretched. Forests of fluttering,

60

grasping, hands reaching out, clawing, trying to get a grip on the man. People's mouths opened in horror as Terry Davey struck his head on the corner of the bottom step.

I was running, forcing my way through the people, desperate to help him. When I reached the steps Thea was down on her knees beside him weeping, shrieking. There was blood running down his face and I knelt beside him and tried to wipe the blood out of his eyes. Thea saw me and shot a hand out, shoving me away. I lost my balance and fell backwards and when I tried to scramble up my ankle gave way.

Thea was standing over me screaming. 'Get away, get away. You freak, you ghoul. Don't touch him. Don't you dare touch him with your filthy Heiney hands. Get away from us before I kill you.'

'I'm sorry, I'm so sorry.' I pleaded, trying desperately to escape, but each time I got halfway up I fell down again. I was so frightened. That was when I saw Shon. She was walking straight towards me through the crowds. She had her arms stretched out to me and she was smiling.

'Evie, Evie, always in trouble, Evie. Come here. It's all right. I'll look after you.'

I wanted so much to be in her arms and I made one last attempt to stand, but then the blackness came down.

61

'Evie? You okay?'A hand tightened around mine - a kind hand, a warm hand, but not hers - not Shon's. Opening my eyes, I see I'm in a car and Dan is at the wheel. He turns his head a fraction and I see his normally smiley mouth is an anxious thin line.

'God, I was getting really worried about you. You keep waking up then going back to sleep again. It might be concussion. I'm taking you to the hospital. Get you checked out. Okay?'

'No. no hospital, I'm fine.'

'You're not.'

'What are you doing here?'

I've got to get you fixed first, then we'll talk.'

'I told you, I'm fine. It's low blood pressure. I faint very easily. I always have.'

'Sure?'

I nodded and shifted in my seat, trying to get comfortable. I attempted to push myself more upright but I wasn't ready for the pain in my ankle. I felt faint and nauseous and buried my head in my lap, waiting for it to pass.

'See,' Dan said, touching my hand. 'That's not normal.'

I pushed his hand away and cautiously raised my head. 'I don't want to go to any hospital.' I prodded my ankle gently and rotated my foot. It didn't hurt too much and the ankle wasn't swollen. 'It's not broken.'

Dan talked while I tried to get my head together. '...You were flaked out, so I just shovelled you into the car, any-old-how.

62

I'm really sorry about your shoe. It must have dropped off when I was carrying you to the car-hire place. You should have seen their faces when I staggered in with an unconscious woman in my arms. I said you were expecting our first and had fainting fits, to make them hurry up with the paper work. It seemed a good idea at the time. They were great but the trouble with me is I get carried away with the story-telling. I told them you had an appointment at the hospital for an ultra-sound and they offered to drive me and wait till you came out and then drive us home. Oh, and by the way, our first baby's going to be called Erhart - after the nice guy from the car-hire place, who filled the tank up for free.'

Dan was silent for a few seconds. 'Sorry, too much talk. I always blather when I'm nervous. Last time we were together you threw a cup of scalding coffee over me. Remember that?'

But I wasn't listening. I was outside the Law Courts again watching a sad old man stumbling down towards a baying pack of newshounds. I saw the women colliding with him and sending him falling, falling, arms and legs splayed, mouth open, long grey hair streaming, until he hit the bottom step, cracking his head open and the blood spattering out like tomato sauce dregs.

'What happened to him? Terry Davey?'

"Dunno. I grabbed you, after that mad woman shoved you over, and ran.'

'Thea?'

'Yup. She went a bit crazy. Understandable in the circumstances.'

63

'I hope he's all right. What were you doing there?'

'Happened to be passing by?'

'Can't you ever give a straight answer to a straight question?'

'What's the point? You think I'm a liar.'

'You are.'

'So? Where d'you want me to drop you off? '

I shrugged.

'Are you staying with someone? A friend or...?'

'...No. '

'So? Where? Your landlord said you'd moved out when I took the bike back.'

'Just drop me off at the station.'

'For God's sake, Evie. You seriously think I'd abandon you in your condition, with only one shoe and a twisted ankle? So, decide where you want me to take you and hurry up about it, or we'll be driving around this God awful one-way system for the rest of our lives.'

'The sea,' I said, saying the first thing that came into my head.

'What?'

'The sea. Noordhoek. I want to go to Noordhoek.' And suddenly I did.

'Okay. I wasn't expecting that.'

'So? It's got to be the railway station then?'

'Hang on. You want to go to the sea, then that's where we'll go. Now, be a pal, sit back and relax. We'll talk later, okay? I'll shout when I need directions. Only I've gotta concentrate on this driving malarkey. Oh my God, not another four-way stop?' He wound the window down and yelled. 'Okay, okay , I saw you, you idiot.'

We joined the rush hour traffic streaming out of the city and were soon on the trunk road that dissected the sprawling settlements of the Cape Flats. We passed crowds of workers going home from their jobs in the city or the massive retail park at Somerset West. There were men and women in smart suits carrying briefcases, side-stepping people pushing bikes and carts, loaded with all manner of goods. There were gangs of women, laughing and jostling each other, many with babies tied to their chests. There were people carrying impossible packages on their heads, these towering parcels defying gravity, while joggers weaved in and out of them like they were sewing giant tacking stitches. There were the old, disabled and plain worn-out people trudging along, heads bent low. Children danced in and out of the long procession and the smoke from cooking fires rose above the settlements like a gauzy curtain.

'Thirsty?' Dan asked, placing a bottle of water in my lap. I didn't touch it and it fell off into the car-well and rolled backwards and forwards until I couldn't stand the noise any longer and picked it up. I drank the whole lot in one long swig. I couldn't remember the last time I'd had water, or food, or sleep. Had I been awake for two years? Is that what was wrong with me?

Finally we turned off the main road and onto Baden Powell Drive, heading towards the coast. At Kommetjie we turned right, skirting the seven km Long Beach. As we drove towards the mountains I could see the hairpin bends of Chapman's Peak Drive, as it reared up in front of us. Dan tapped the windscreen and I followed the lazy drifting shape of a black eagle, pinned like a dead butterfly to the shimmering pearly opalescence of the evening sky.

*

When we were kids Ma and Dad used to rent a beach house along this stretch of coast. Dad commuted to his law firm in Cape Town from here. We always booked the same house. I loved that place. The smell of salt at the front door and the sun-bleached wooden floors. It was our special, secret place and once, when we were packing up to go back to Stellenbosch, the next people, who were renting it, arrived early and their kids ran around claiming their rooms and bringing their stuff in. We hated them. None of us children spoke on the way home and Ma and Dad had a flaming row about him driving too fast. Stupid, the things you remember.

There was a civet who lived on the roof of the seaside house - he used to peer over the guttering at us as we sat on the veranda playing cards in the evening. We would nudge each other and put our fingers to our lips, frightened of scaring him away and his black panda eyes and white fur face would hang there in the

66

darkness like the Cheshire Cat's. He used to eat the remnants of chips and fruit we dropped and by the morning the floor would be spotless again.

I don't know why we stopped coming. I suppose we got to the age where we wanted to do our own thing. When I think back it was probably around that time when my parents' marriage started to go wrong. We, of course, were too busy tackling our own hormonal fireworks to worry about them.

*

The beach houses were on Dan's side and I had to sit forward in my seat to get a good view. I thought I might recognise the one that had been ours.

'D'you want me to stop somewhere?' Dan asked.

I shook my head. I gave up looking after a while. Like everywhere else on this coast there had been a lot of building development. Most of the older wooden houses had been pulled down and modern brick monstrosities erected in their place. There was a Camelot in pink brick, numerous haciendas, a Rapunzel castle and at least three thatched cottages.

We'd liked this stretch of beach because it had never been as busy as the more popular Cape Town resorts like Simon's Town or Boulder Beach, where the African penguins hung out. The sea at Long Beach was rough and the water chilly but it was great for body-boarding and surfing. Sometimes we used to hire ponies and gallop the whole length of the beach down to Kommetjie and back to Noordhoek, which was a pretty little village at the foot of

Chapman's Peak. That was where we bought milk-tart and sweets and buckets and spades.

Dan drove on into the soft night and eventually, just before we reached Noordhoek, I pointed out a track on our left and he turned onto it and followed it down to a promontory of rock where we parked. Dan cut the engine, then got out and lit up. I watched as the glow from his cigarette danced from mouth to hand, like a firefly. I followed him slowly, holding onto the door handle until I was sure my ankle could take my weight. I stood still for a moment letting the darkness wrap itself around me and then I limped down the path towards the sea.

Dan's voice followed me. 'Hang on, Evie and I'll give you a hand.'

'No, I'm okay, thanks.' This was my beach and I knew every rock and pothole on that path.

There was a channel of fast moving water, slicing down the side of the headland, where I'd learnt to swim. It was protected from the open sea and the great whites that patrolled like hungry vultures just beyond a bolster of rocks. When I reached the beach I flopped down, pushed off my sandal and pressed my toes into the cool sand. It felt so good. I touched my ankle gently. It was a bit sore and slightly puffy but I was sure there was nothing broken. There was no wind and the water lapped gently on the shingle. I heard Dan slipping down the path behind me and his *shit* as he stubbed his toe on a rock.

He sank down beside me and lay out flat, his arms stretched behind his head. The Southern Cross hung above us, so bright and clear it seemed as if it might drop out of the sky on top of us. I felt my eyelids drooping but Dan sat up and tossed a pebble high into the air. We heard the 'plop' as it hit the water further out. 'So?' he said leaning on one elbow and looking down at me. 'I think we should talk.'

'I'm tired, Dan.'

'Are you in love with him?'

That woke me up. 'What?'

'Simple question. Are you in love with Viktor Heiney?'

'Are you crazy?'

'Well, why else would you have spent the last year and a half following his case?'

'My 'good 'friends' been talking have they?'

'What d'you expect? You're famous and they're journalists. God, how they'd love to do a double-spread on you.'

'Well that's okay isn't it, because you beat them to it.'

'You're way off the mark.'

'I know you're writing about Shon, so that means you're writing about me too.'

'No, I'm not.'

'I don't believe you.'

'Believe what you want, Evie. All I want is to understand what this is all about.'

'Why? It's none of your business.'

He sighed heavily. 'God. You're a difficult woman.'

'No one asked you to get involved. I didn't encourage you.'

'True.'

' But, if you must know, I've been studying Heiney.'

'Of course you have.'

'I'm writing a book about him. Isn't that what all us hacks do?'

I'd never been much good at sarcasm and he snorted and sat up, brushing the sand out of his hair. 'What are you going to do for excitement now he's going to prison?'

'Excitement? Is that what you call it?'

'It's over, Evie.'

'Never.'

He tried to take my hand but I snatched it away. 'He thinks he's got away with it. Five years for slaughtering a defenceless woman, the woman he says he worshipped. Five years for blowing her brains out and he won't do the full term, everyone knows that. He'll be out on parole in a few months, safe in his shiny millionaire's mansion, surrounded by his loving family and adoring public.'

'The thing is, Evie, Heiney might be telling the truth. Maybe it really was an accident. He's had a fair trial and the judge did what she could with the evidence. It's the way your legal system works and there's nothing you can do about it.'

'I can do plenty.' I whispered.

'What?'

'I want to go home.'

'Home? Where's that then?'

'Please.'

'We've only just got here for God's sake.' He grasped my hand and when I tried to pull it away he gripped tighter. 'Why are you doing this to yourself? D'you think you have to be punished for something, to suffer like Shon suffered? He's not Nick Ground, Evie. He's not the man who murdered your sister.'

I tried to scramble to my feet but I couldn't, so I turned onto my knees and crawled away. But Dan was beside me, lifting me up, cradling my head against his shoulder. 'It's alright. I can help you if you'll let me. Please let me.'

'No, no one can help me. It's too late.'

He ran his finger down my face wiping away my tears and rocking me in his arms.

'I promised her. I have to keep my promise.'

'What did you promise? Evie?'

I shook my head.

He started to say something but sighed and held out his hands, palms flat, as if he was surrendering. 'Okay, I'll take you home tomorrow, where ever that is, but now we're going to sleep. We can doss down in the car. I've got some sandwiches and stuff.'

'I'll sleep here. '

'Indeed you will not.'

'Why?'

'There are wild animals.'

'Like what?'

'Crocodiles, hippos, sharks...'

'...The wildest animal around here is a meerkat, Dan, or a tortoise or an otter - if you're really lucky.'

'Okay, you win, but I've got a few calls to make. Can't get reception down here, should be better up on the road. I'll see you in a few minutes.'

After he'd gone I lay down on the sand again and closed my eyes. Taking a deep, deep breath I let it out very slowly and felt my heart rate gradually slow down.

I woke once in the night with cramp in my foot and when I turned over to ease it I found Dan asleep beside me. His fluttering breath tickled my face. He lay curled up with one arm flung behind his head like a child. I envied him that capacity to let go, belong to the sleeping and dreaming. Go there fearlessly. He smelt so good and I wanted to move into the crook of his arm. He wouldn't even know I was there. It had been such a long time since anyone had held me with tenderness. But I couldn't do it and I turned away.

*

We were in the big department store in Cape Town, going up the escalator. Shon was in front with Ma, who was trying to wriggle out of her grasp, but Shon had her tight. I stood close behind, with my hand on Ma's bum, propelling her upwards. We were all laughing.

'Stop, stop,' Ma squealed between hiccups of laughter. 'I'll wet myself if you don't let me go.'

'Do you promise to submit to our will and try on some fascinators for your daughter's graduation?'

'But I don't want a fascinator,' she wailed, 'I hate hats and I loathe bloody fascinators.'

Shon looked sternly at Ma. 'Mother, language. Please, not in front of the children.'

I presume she meant me.

'Your fear of hats must be psychological, Mrs Adze. We need to get to the bottom of this phobia. Did you have a nasty experience with a hat in your youth?'

By the time we reached the top we were hysterical. We stood in a row doubled up. The other shoppers gave us a wide birth. I didn't blame them. One of us would nearly get control of themselves, but then she'd look at the other two and start all over again. Ma was laughing so much she had tears streaming down her face.

'Please, I beg of you, no more. Look, let's have a coffee and discuss this like rational human beings.' That set us off again and our laughter got louder and louder until suddenly it wasn't funny anymore, because now it was a blood-curdling shriek.

*

I woke with a start but the shrieking was still in my head and it was getting louder and closer. I stared around but all I saw was the sand and sea. The wind had strengthened in the night and my hair whipped across my face. It was cold and a watery sun was emerging from the grey sea. I rubbed at my eyes but all I managed to do was get sand in them. I could only open them a crack and that's when I saw something sweeping towards me across the water.

The shrieking laughter came again and I tried to run, but my ankle buckled and I fell back onto the sand. A huge black shape was coming straight for me, arms outstretched, mouth open, screaming and screaming. There was something dangling from its mouth, some sort of twisting, gyrating, silver snake. I was frantic now and I crouched on the sand with my arms covering my head. I felt the draught of air as the thing skimmed low over my head, showering me with droplets of water.

I was sobbing and then Dan was beside me and I clung to him. 'Please, don't let it...please...'

' Evie, it's okay. It's okay. It's only a bird. A bloody great big one I grant you but still a bird. What did you think it was? Evie open your eyes. Look, it's flying inland, taking a fish back to its fledglings. Quick before it disappears.'

I opened my eyes just in time to see it flying into the line of trees behind the beach.

'Oh wow. Amazing. Look at it go, Evie. What an incredible sight.'

'A sea eagle,' I muttered, the fear draining out of me. Not a ghost or a creature from hell - just a bird.

'You're kidding me.' Dan ran up the beach, pulling out his cell as he ran. 'No one's gonna believe this back home.' He snapped away and then came back to me smiling. 'And you're absolutely sure that's what it was? I nodded. Thank you, God,' he shouted, arms reaching up to the sky. 'My first, gorgeous, amazing African sea eagle. The span on it? It must have been, what? Seven, eight feet wide?'

My teeth were chattering now. I was so cold.

'Hey, come here,' he said. "There was a cafe open in Noordhoek. They get up early in that place. D'you want this?' and he held out a polystyrene cup. Steam was coming up through the lip.

My hand brushed his as I took it.

'You're not gonna throw that over me or anything are you?' He was smiling but his eyes were wary. 'Get that down you, then we'll go find some food. I'm starving.'

I held the cup in both hands relishing the warmth. 'Thanks, Dan.'

'You're welcome.' He looked so pleased with himself.

Talking

It was true, Dan was very hungry. I had to suffer his meat frenzy in silence. I only looked away once when he bit into his emu steak-burger and the juices dribbled down his chin. Gross. I attempted an omelette with mushrooms. I knew he was watching me as I ate, like some worried parent with a picky child. Each mouthful was a minor triumph but the swallowing was something else.

When we were back on the road Dan was serious again. We didn't talk, but the air was heavy with all those unspoken thoughts. It felt like the prickly heat before a storm. Dan tuned the wireless onto some anodyne music station and I was drifting off to sleep when the music was interrupted by a news flash. It was about Terry Davey. His head injuries were so severe, he'd been put into an induced coma. The prognosis wasn't good but he was in the best neurological unit in Cape Town. There was no way he had health insurance so some anonymous benefactor must be footing the bill. No prizes for guessing who that was. Blood money? I know what I'd have done with it but there was a huge amount of support for Terry Davey and I didn't begrudge him any of it. After all, he couldn't run his business now and the long trial must have eaten up any savings he once had. Rachel Davey had been supporting her father for years. The bulletin said his niece was at his bedside and the old man wasn't expected to survive the night. I was just taking in this information when there was a report about V.

76

'Leave it,' I said, as Dan leant forward to switch off.

'It's finished, Evie. The guy's in prison. What more d'you want?"

'I want to hear this.'

'For God's sake.'

'Please, Dan. It's...important.' I tried to keep my voice steady.

He pulled off the main road onto the hard shoulder and jammed on the brakes He got out of the car, slammed the door and walked away and stood with his back to me, talking into his cell.

V had started his prison sentence in Cape Town's maximum Security Prison. It was a tough and dangerous place. Not only was it overcrowded but it housed some of South Africa's most violent criminals. The report went on to describe what V's life would be like inside. He would be allowed two visitors a week and no physical contact with family or friends. Any treat had to be bought at the prison 'tuck shop'. I knew it was his birthday in a few days time so I tweeted Melanie to say I was sending some money to buy something from the prison store for his birthday. I would send a card and a small amount of rand in an envelope to her. I asked her to forward a tweet to V from me. *'Dear V, Thinking of you. May God protect you from your friend E.'* I left out that comma on purpose.

After this, the chief prosecutor of the case was interviewed. They were preparing an appeal against V's sentence. If successful, the case would be heard by three judges in the Supreme Court later this year. A successful outcome would be a much longer custodial sentence but, in all probability, V could be out of prison and on parole before it even got to the Supreme Court. I needed to know what was going to happen, otherwise how could I make my plan? It was like a game of chess and I didn't know which piece to move next. I needed to be on my own to work it all out.

At the end of the bulletin I switched off and waited. Dan stubbed out his cigarette and got back in the car. 'So? Where to?'

'The railway station.'

'For Chrissake, Evie. I'm taking you to a proper address or you can get out now.'

'No one asked you to interfere in my life.'

'True. But then I'm a bloody idiot, aren't I?'

'I don't know what you are.'

'Maybe that's because you've not interested. If you want I could bore you for days about me, my family, what school I went to, how many girlfriend's I've had - that wouldn't take long. Just ask. '

'Are you never serious?'

'Not if I can help it.'

'Did Frankie send you to spy on me yesterday?'

'I was doing my job. Reporting for the paper. What was your excuse?'

'How did you know I was there?'

He laughed out loud at that. 'Oh please. Not again. I know, we know, everyone knows where you've been spending your vacations.'

'It's nobody's business what I do.'

'True.'

'They don't care.'

'Maybe not, but I do.'

It was my turn to laugh. 'You? You just wanted a good story.'

He was quiet for a moment. 'Yeah, well why else would I be putting myself out for someone who's so full of self-pity she hasn't got time for anyone but herself?'

I didn't like the way this conversation was going. 'You want to know where I live? It's Marine Drive - number 201, Stellenbosch. Can we go now, please?'

'No.'

'You said you'd take me. You promised, but then, I know what a liar you are.'

He leant across me and flung open my door. 'Okay. Have it your own way. Get out.'

I thought he was kidding but he wasn't smiling. 'But we're in the middle of nowhere. I don't have any money, Dan, and it's a long way.'

'Tough.'

'You promised.'

'But I'm a liar aren't I?'

'Please, Dan. I'm sorry.'

He banged his head on the steering wheel. 'Oh God, Evie. Shut the friggin' door. Right. Cards on the table. This isn't about Viktor Heiney at all, is it? This is about Nick Ground, the bastard who murdered your sister. He was never caught and you want to see someone pay for her death - doesn't matter who - correct? '

'What are you? An amateur psychiatrist? I...I'm interested, that's all.'

'You mean it's like a hobby? You collect gruesome murders?'

'My father's a criminal lawyer, I grew up with it. Maybe it's in the blood.'

He ignored me, 'So, this is what's gonna happen. I'll take you home, but first you have to tell me what really happened the day you found your sister.'

'I don't talk about that.'

'But now you're going to.'

'No.'

'Did you like him, Evie? Nick Ground? Were you jealous of your sister? Is that it? He was a movie star and he was Shon's boyfriend but you wanted him? And now all you're left with is guilt?'

He was ready for me and grabbed my wrist before I could hit him. 'Always so violent, Evie.'

'I hate you. How could you even think something like that? It's obscene. I loved my sister.'

'Yeh, well sorry, but it wouldn't be the first time siblings fell in love with the same person. I just want you to understand what's making you like this.'

'Can't you just leave me alone?'

'Don't you think I've considered that?'

'I didn't ask you to help me.'

'No, you didn't. So? Start talking and then I'll take you home and you needn't ever see me again.'

'You already know what happened, the whole world knows, so don't expect me to repeat it for you to drool over. Go online. It's all there, every disgusting, pornographic detail.'

'But that's the point, Evie, it's not all there. You saw something no one should ever see, and somehow you have to deal with it...It's the only way to survive.'

'Maybe I don't want to survive?'

'That's a terrible thing to say.'

'D'you think I want to be like this? That I don't want to be normal? I can't forget it, Dan. I never will. The person I loved more than anything in the world was slaughtered, like a...used animal, and I found her.'

'I know how hard it is, Evie, but if you keep it all trapped in your head you really will go mad and then Nick Ground will have killed you too.'

'I'm dead already.'

'Evie. Please. Tell me what happened.'

'I'll hate you if you make me.'

'That's a risk I have to take.'

He sat motionless, staring out at the cars as they flashed by on the highway, and I knew I had no choice.

It all began

I cleared my throat and tried to speak but the words felt like mud in my mouth. Dan handed me the water bottle and I took several large gulps. He waited patiently until, at last, I was able to get the words out. 'I don't know where to begin.'

Tell me about yourself, back then. What were you doing?'

'Working on the paper.'

'Doing what? Coffee girl?'

'I'd just landed my first small column.'

'Impressive.'

'The 'eating out' piece - 500 words and one pic for the Friday edition. My big break. 'A hundred ways to braai wors.' I saw Dan's mouth twitch. 'I know it doesn't sound much but if I did okay Frankie promised me 'something' on the news desk. I'd have swum with great whites for the chance of reporting real news.' I was talking too fast and I made a conscious effort to slow down.

'The Chronicle' was my first job after uni. Ma was really pleased for me, so was Shon, but Dad was disappointed. He made all the right noises but he didn't mean it. I was supposed to go into the family law firm with him and Shon but I wasn't cut out to be a lawyer and besides, I didn't get the grades. No, Shon was the high roller in our family. She got a double first. The sky was the limit for my sister.

All I'd ever been good at was writing. I kept a notebook for my scribblings and read so much it made my eyes ache. Even when I was a little kid Ma knew where to find me when I was supposed to be doing my chores. There I'd be under the oak tree reading. I loved a good cry. Dogs being mistreated, children being orphaned, cruel stepmothers. I loved it. As I got older I went to the theatre as much as I could and acted in all the High School productions. I usually got the mad, bad, crazy-woman parts like *Lady Macbeth,* or the first *Mrs Rochester,* or the demented old bird in Lorca's *Blood Wedding.* The best part I ever played was *Medea.* God, I loved that woman. No one put her down and lived to tell the tale. Jason discovered the hard way. Remember? Medea and the poison dress for Jason's new woman. Brilliant.'

Dan smiled. 'Yeh, I can see why she would have appealed to you.'

I let that go.

'You're a good writer, Evie. Frankie was very pleased with your articles about Mandela. She was gutted she had to let you go.'

'Yeh, well...'

'...I've got a copy of the piece. Maybe you'd like to see it some time? So? What did you work on before the food column?'

'The usual stuff, weddings, funerals, kid's parties, flower festivals, minor celebrity functions and, if I was really lucky, road accidents. At least I didn't have to eat anything at those. I would have puked if I'd been offered another braai. I'm a vegetarian for God's sake. But now I could use irony and humour to demonise

84

South Africa's national obsession with burnt meat. I had thought of calling that first article, 'The worst of wors,' but Frankie gave me one of her raised eyebrow looks. Has she done that with you yet?'

'Yup, all the time.'

I was quiet for a bit after that. I knew what came next. Dan was very patient and eventually I took a deep breath and began.

'It was the Friday we'd arranged to take Ma out for her birthday meal and I was hurrying to finish off my article. Trouble was I'd gone off on a tangent about the importance of food in children's fairy stories, like *Hansel and Gretel* and *Charlie and the Chocolate factory* and *The Tiger who came to Tea*. I was struggling to edit 2,000 words down to 500. Anyway, by the time I finished I'd missed the train to Stellenbosch. The next one wasn't due for another hour so I decided to get a taxi to Shon's and drive over with her. I could pick up Ma's flowers and fizz on the way. Shon, me and Jane – our 'baby' sister – had clubbed together to buy them a weekend away in Hermanus - posh hotel, the works. It was the Whale Festival and the town would be buzzing. Ma was into Cape jazz and most of the seafront bars and restaurants had live music. She would love it.

I was really looking forward to seeing Shon. We hadn't had a proper gossip for ages and I would have her to myself because her boyfriend, Nick Ground, was shooting the latest episode in a television mini-series about pirates. Nick was drop-dead gorgeous - blond hair, intense blue eyes, amazing bone structure, lovely body. I'd seen one episode of the series and it was pretty crap but Nick looked amazing in it and he was getting a whole lot of media coverage. The South African movie industry was making mega bucks and Nick Ground was all set for a golden future.

Shon was my sister but she was also my best friend. I'd grown up in her shadow but, unbelievably, we were still mates. At school, at home, socially, she was the one everyone remembered. I should have hated her, well I had, a bit, in my teens, when I still had a brace on my teeth and no boobs. I can't remember a time when she didn't have a trail of boyfriends buzzing around her like male bees after the Queen.

I glanced at Dan. I didn't want him to get the wrong idea about Shon.

'My sister wasn't just beautiful. She was passionate about loads of stuff, especially violence against women and was making a name for herself in the criminal courts, in rape and domestic violence cases. She also gave her professional services free at rape crisis centres and women's refuges, all over The Cape.'

Dan nodded. 'Yeh, I've read about it.'

'She built up a rapport with a lot of top broadsheet journalists and allowed herself to be photographed and interviewed with Nick, as his glamorous girlfriend, and in exchange they ran articles on women's issues and publicised forthcoming protest campaigns. In fact the day after it happened she and I were going on a march here in Cape Town against rape, only...'

Dan jumped in. '...Yeh, wasn't she campaigning for government funding to provide rape-testing kits in police stations? There has to be evidence or the abusers usually walks free. The stats are horrific. What is it? Out of the 50,000 rape cases reported to the police last year – that works out to something like one rape a minute - there have only been 4,500 convictions?'

'Yeah. Shon loved all the women she helped, really loved them. They were her friends. She was so kind but it took its toll. I think sometimes she got too involved. D'you know what I mean? I remember one time when I called in at her office and found her slumped in the chair. She looked terrible. Her mouth was wide with shock and her beautiful face was ashen and drawn, I was so frightened. I thought she was having a heart attack or something. '...*Two years old,* she kept muttering, '...*two years old and the bastards raped her and left her to die on the tip*.'

'I never knew what to say when something like that happened. It was horrific for me but it was a hundred times worse for her.' I hesitated and looked at Dan, 'D'you know she had an abortion when she was seventeen?'

'Yeh.'

'In the papers?'

He nodded. Did she tell Nick Ground about it?'

I shrugged. 'I don't know. Probably not. He came from a very religious background. I don't think his family would have approved.'

'Did you meet his parents?'

'No. They were in the diplomatic service and had a place in a massive house on the coast near Port Elizabeth. Nick was a perfect gentleman, had good manners, nice clothes, Ma liked him a lot. I liked him too, to begin with, but I was surprised at how he treated Shon sometimes, you know, off hand, as if he didn't care. Apparently he'd lived all over Europe as a child and went to a British public school, which he loathed. He'd been brought up by his grandparents who doted on him. He was the only grandchild and Shon said they spoilt him, so he was used to getting his own way.

When Shon told me they might try for a baby I was glad for her. I knew how desperately she wanted a child, so it surprised me when, not long after this, she said she'd changed her mind. *'Nick's never grown up,'* she explained, and I remember her wry smile. *'I'd have two infants to look after, not one.'* I wanted to ask her about it but Nick walked in on us and I think he must have heard because he seemed angry - not his usual charming self. He made it clear he wanted me to leave. He was pretty rude actually and I was a bit hurt. Up till then he and I'd got on great. We used to talk about the books and films we loved. He even promised he'd get me a part in his next film.

Anyway, on my way out I said *'Okay, see you soon,'* looking at Shon but she was staring at Nick. I know this is in retrospect but I'm sure she was scared.'

*

I blew my nose and took another long drink - anything to delay what I had to say next. I kept my eyes down as I spoke.

'The night of Ma's birthday I arrived at Shon's place by taxi, just as the sun was setting. It was beautiful. I backed out of the taxi carefully, so I wouldn't damage the bouquet. It was huge, much too big really, but Shon had ordered it and my sister was never a woman to do things by half.

Shon and Nick's apartment was in a modern, elegant glass and chrome building overlooking the sea. Once inside you felt as if you were underwater - surrounded on three sides by the blue sea and sky. I dread to think what the rent was. However, Shon was a top flight lawyer now and Nick must be earning shed-loads of rand. Even Dad was impressed with the place and had visited them a few times. I was quite surprised, because he didn't normally like people who flaunted their wealth.

I hadn't texted Shon to let her know I was coming because I expected her to be there, so I was surprised when I buzzed her intercom and there was no answer. On the ground floor there was an area run by a very friendly and efficient lady during the day but she wasn't there by the time I arrived. A male security guard was on duty. He insisted on taking down my details and checking up on his computer, making me wait for quite some time before he okayed me. There was no one else there so maybe he just wanted to fill in some time. Eventually he relaxed a bit and we chatted about rugby – what else? I sat in one of the deep leather chairs and flicked through a magazine. Guess who was on the front page? The guard knew about Nick and I promised to get him an autograph some time.

He made me a coffee while I rang Shon. She must be on her way back from work by now. It went to her voice mail.

'Hi, Shon. Where are you? I'm at yours, missed the bloody train. Is it okay if I come with you? Hope everything's okay. See you. Oh, and I picked up the flowers and stuff. Put your skates on, hey?'

If she was in court she wouldn't be able to use her phone. I rang Jane, just in case Shon and I were late. My little sister had turned into a scary mother of two. *'Well, for, Chrissake!* ' she yelled, over the din one of her twins was making. *'I can be on time and I've got a husband and two children to organise! Where is she? '*

'At work?' I suggested.

Jane didn't do irony. *'Of course she's at work. I mean why couldn't she plan her day better? And why are you there? You should be on your way home by now.'*

'For God's sake, Jane. Just hold the fort till we get there, okay? Think you can do that?'

She snorted and switched off. I hated it when she did that. She was always putting the phone down on me. One of these days I'd have it out with her, but not today. I looked at the time. Come on, Shon.

I had a pass key to her apartment so I decided to go up. At least I could watch the telly up there, make myself a drink. And it crossed my mind that she might be up there already. The guy on the desk said he hadn't seen her come in but maybe she'd come in before he arrived. Perhaps she was having a sleep. I knew how exhausted she got when she was working on a case. Yes, that would be it.

So, I cleared it with the guard and headed for the glass-sided lift. As the door closed a spike of deep crimson gladioli was trapped and an explosion of petals arced down onto the beautiful gold-flecked marble flooring. Funny how trivial things stick in your head. I can still see that line of red and I remember thinking how pretty it looked.

Shon and Nick's place was way up on the fifteenth floor, so I had time to admire the view as I drifted upwards. I was really excited about seeing Shon. There was so much I wanted to talk to her about and questions to ask and secrets to share and jokes, and everything. I never got the opportunity to gossip now. I liked Nick but he was always there demanding attention. Maybe that's what movie stars get like - twitchy in case someone steals their thunder?

Dumping the flowers and booze on the floor I slid the key card in. 'Shon?' I called, as the door quietly shut behind me. 'Shon? Are you there? It's me.' I didn't want to spook her. She'd always been a bit nervous when she was on her own. She'd had a couple of nasty break-ins in her other flat, that's why it was so good that she was in such a safe place now. It was getting dark and the setting sun was turning the turquoise sea into a gilded opaque mirror. Windows stretched from floor to ceiling in the open-plan hallway. There was a spiral staircase leading up to the mezzanine floor from the hall where the bedrooms and bathrooms were. Then there was another smaller flight of stairs leading up to the living area and kitchen. The views over the waterfront were to-die-for. Fabulous. I was so envious.

I didn't need to turn any lights on. Everything was highlighted in a beautiful golden, shimmering glow. It was absolutely quiet except for the sound of running water from upstairs. So, that was it, she was having a shower. 'Shon?' My voice echoed up the stairwell. There was an elegant leather sofa at the foot of the stairs and I sank down into it, easing off my shoes. It was cool inside the flat. Every sound was magnified a thousand times by the space. The architect had known what he was doing. The interior was lit by the sky and the sea, which was changing into molten metal as the sun went down

'Shon?' Silence, except for that incessant *drip, drip, drip.*

Maybe Nick was here after all. Maybe they were sharing a shower. God! That would be so embarrassing. I flipped open my phone and texted Shon. I didn't want to walk in on them. *'Hi, Are u there? I'm downstairs. Sorry If... but we should get going asap. J's on the warpath!'* I heard the text alert tone ringing somewhere above me. So, she was here. I could imagine her scrambling into

92

her clothes, giggling. So much for Nick working. He must have got home early. I felt a stab of disappointment but I shook it off and settled back in the chair, flicking through a magazine. It was one of Shon's campaign pamphlets. There was a big piece about domestic violence in South Africa and an article by someone from the Medical Research Council. It was well written. *'We live in a deeply patriarchal and injured society where the rights of women are not respected.'* Then there were harrowing photos of women who'd been attacked by their partners. It was dark now and I jumped up and switched on all the lights. I wished there were curtains to draw. I felt exposed. Anyone could look in. Stupid. I was fifteen floors up, looking out to sea, who could see me?

I rang Jane, again.

'Yes? What?'

I kept my voice friendly. *'Hi, look there's been a bit of a hitch. You take Ma and Dad to the restaurant and we'll catch up with you there.'*

'Dad's gonna go ape.'

'Tough' I snapped. *'It's Ma's birthday and she'll understand.'* Jane started to protest but I cut her off. *' See you there, we'll be as quick as we can.'* I talked fast, so she couldn't interrupt and then I switched off first. How good was that?

I started up the stairs to the mezzanine. Surely they'd be dressed by now. I hesitated on the third step and peered upwards. I could see that most of the doors up there were open and one was banging. 'The Cape Doctor' was blowing hard tonight. The sound

93

of running water was louder. I went up to the top and stood outside the bathroom door. The floor was sopping wet. I'd never used a wet room but I was sure it wasn't supposed to leak. There was a tide line that was widening and widening and starting to drip down the stairwell. I banged loudly on the door. 'Shon? You there? I'm coming in, ready or not.' No answer so I went inside. The room was full of steam but I could see it was empty. I splashed across to the taps and switched off the water.

Shon's bedroom door was the one that was banging. My fingers were trembling as I knocked, *'Shon?'* I waited a moment then pushed the door and went inside. It was totally dark. The heavy drapes were pulled. I knew the bed was in front of the window but I couldn't understand why the curtains were drawn because Shon loved to lie there and watch the sea. She had rigged up a telescope by the bed, so she could watch the Southern Right whales and their calves and sometimes see the dorsal fins of great whites and pods of dolphins playing around the whales.

My eyes were getting used to the dark now and I saw there was a shape on the bed - just one - a woman's shape. I took a step closer and whispered, *'Shon? Wake up. It's me, Evie.'* She didn't move. *'You okay?'* She was on her back and twisted somehow. It was all wrong. I tried to stay calm. Maybe she was ill. Her long blonde hair was across her face and I touched her arm but she didn't move... '

Dan reached over and laid his hand on mine. I was trembling. 'I can't,' I said. 'Please, don't make me.'

'You must, Evie, I'm sorry but you must.'

And he was right. Not much longer now. I was nearly done and after a few moments I continued.

'So, I...So, I switched on the bedside lamp and made myself look. Shon's head was thrown back on the pillow and her hands were clenched at her throat. There was something tied around her neck – a scarf – something soft with a knot in it, against her windpipe. I tried to untie it, it must be hurting her, and it came loose after a moment or two. No, not a scarf, a wispy pair of pants in silky, sexy, lurid purple. The knot was where the crotch was.

I pushed the hair away from her face and saw that it was covered in blood. There were streaks of it coming from her eyes and down her ears. Her mouth hung slackly open and she was staring at me. *'Shon? Wake up. I'm here, it's all right. Please.'* She was naked and her long legs were wide open. I touched her arm gently. She was so cold. I grabbed the duvet and pulled it up to cover her, to make her warm, then I lay down beside her, my arms wrapped around her.

'Please, Shon. Don't do this. Say something. Please...don't be dead, don't. It's not real. You're not dead', and I shook her so hard I was frightened I'd hurt her. 'No, no, you mustn't do this. Open your eyes.'

Remembering

I kept my eyes shut on the drive back to Stellenbosch. I wanted Dan to think I was asleep so that he wouldn't talk. And all the time my body was screaming out for sleep. I desperately needed to slide into oblivion but my brain had other ideas. I had to stay awake. I had to remember.

*

The little I remember of what happened after I found Shon is random and in no sequential order. Ma and Dad were there and Jane too. She was screaming and screaming and I wanted to yell at her to stop but I had no voice. I was so cold and someone put a big blanket over my shoulders. It felt itchy, maybe it was a rug. I pulled it right over my head so that I didn't have to look at anyone, or see them carrying Shon down that spiral staircase. I heard the paramedics stumbling and grunting as they manhandled the stretcher around the bends. *'Is it real? Is this really happening?'* and someone said. *'Yes, it's real. I'm sorry.'*

I had to answer questions when the cops arrived. Ma was beside me, stroking my hand, and when she thought they'd asked me enough she made them stop. She was so calm. I can't remember how Dad reacted but I've got this picture in my head of him standing in a corner, with his back to us, talking into his cell phone. He was in a very smart suit, a big, handsome man. He didn't look his age. Ma had been to the hairdressers and her brown hair was swept up in a complicated chignon. She smelt so nice. She always wore the same perfume. I can't remember what it was but I always associated that smell with her. when she was smiling and happy, in a pretty dress, going out somewhere with Dad. Several strands of her hair had come adrift and she kept tucking them behind her ears. She was beautiful and I clung to her hand. That may have been the last time we touched each other with any level of feeling.

The cops asked what time I'd arrived, why was I there, what did I talk about to the security guy, what was he like? Stupid questions. Why were they wasting time talking about the guard when they should be out there, checking the airports and putting up road and rail blocks, catching Nick Ground. I never once considered it could have been anyone else. I didn't need the pathologist's report and I was right. An open and shut case, but it wasn't, was it? It never is. They took the security guard in for questioning later because they thought Nick may have bribed him not to say anything. They even pulled in the lovely lady who worked the day shift. She said Shon came home just before she knocked off and was her normal friendly self. They talked about the march in Cape Town the next day and Shon asked if she was going but the woman had to work. Shon told her that Nick was filming and wouldn't be in till much later and that we were taking Ma out for her birthday. Nick must have sneaked in between her knocking off and the guard coming on for his shift. Or maybe he'd been there all the time, waiting.

I expected Nick Ground to be arrested quickly, we all did. His DNA was everywhere at the crime scene. There was irrefutable forensic evidence. No one else was in the frame. Nick Ground had raped and murdered my sister, so why wasn't he caught? How could he just disappear off the face of the earth? He's been spotted all over the world - Switzerland, Brazil, Russia, the Baltic States - but nothing has ever come of it. Dad hired a private detective after Interpol drew a blank. Nothing. And for us, her family and friends, the false leads and false hopes gradually dribbled away into bitter frustration and rage. I'll never know what really happened to Shon that night, or what she was thinking, or how scared she must have been. That's what I have nightmares about, my Shon being terrified.

His parents were out of the country the night it happened, attending a summit on global warming in Frankfurt and were flying back that night. I saw them being interviewed. They looked terrible. I tried to hate them but I couldn't. They were as shocked as everyone else. They couldn't, wouldn't believe their son was a murderer.

When they searched the apartment none of his stuff had been taken, except his passport and credit cards and when the cops contacted the film studios they discovered he hadn't been working for a fortnight. His contract had been terminated. He was a liability - a druggie.

But the nightmare didn't end there because the cops found tik in the apartment - a lot of it. I was shocked, we all were. Shon hated drugs and especially tik. It was cheap - R20/ R30 a straw - and easy to buy. It was aimed at kids and made the user euphoric and sexually potent. We had the lecture from Ma when it first hit the streets back in the early 2000s. She warned us so many times we could have quoted it by heart. *'Tik affects the central nervous system releasing dopamine into the brain that influences emotions and sensations of pleasure and pain. Users can have intensely pleasurable highs that can last for twelve hours. It not only increases libido but allows the user to have sex for much longer periods of time. The end result? Fewer inhibitions, more sexual partners. The tik user could have sex without guilt or the distractions of shame or embarrassment.'*

'Just imagine,' Shon laughed, rolling her eyes, when Ma was out of earshot.

They said Shon was a user too. I tried to keep it from Ma but in the end it was inevitable that she found out. *'Murdered model was tik addict.'* I just couldn't believe it, it had to be a mistake. Shon knew the appalling effects of this drug on people. She'd seen it first hand, seen how it made some users psychotic and violent and the horrible consequences. It was also to blame for spreading HIV through the townships. Shon would never have used it. I would have staked my life on that.

But dear Jane put me right. 'The pathologist's report is indisputable, Evie. It was in her bloodstream.'

'He must have forced her.'

'Really? How d'you do that, exactly? You smoke the stuff through a straw, pressed against a heated light bulb.' She shrugged. 'Hard to force someone to do that, don't you think?'

She saw my look and sighed heavily. 'Yeah. I know it's hard to believe. Our sister was so perfect wasn't she? But I have to be more practical than you, Evie. This is about damage limitation for me. I have to protect my children. The sooner we can all accept what's happened and put it behind us, get back to normal, the better. She made a mistake. Live with it.'

I don't know how I didn't punch her.

And as usual she had to have the last word. 'She wasn't the angel you thought she was, Evie.. People talk, you know...'

'No...' I shouted, jabbing my finger at her. 'People don't talk...you talk, you open that vicious slash of a mouth of yours and poison spews out.'

'Yeah ,' she sighed and walked away. 'Whatever.'

Ma wouldn't believe Shon had used tik either. It hadn't happened, full stop, end of story. Maybe it was easier for her to push it to the back of her mind because there was nothing she could do about it. Shon was an adult.

We were still dealing with that bombshell when something else happened. The first I knew about it was when Ma burst into my bedroom one morning, and flung a newspaper down in front of me.

'Did you know about this, Evie?'

I glanced at the headlines, 'Movie Star's murdered girlfriend in abortion scandal.' My sleep-fuddled brain was trying to grasp what was happening. Where in God's name had they dredged that up from? And what on earth did it have to do with my sister's murder? But even as I thought it, I knew the tenaciousness of the media. Anything to sell newspapers. Ma was staring at me but I couldn't look her in the eye.

'She had an abortion and you knew?' Ma whispered. 'You knew and you never told me?'

'Ma,' I began, 'Shon made me promise. She didn't want to upset you...'

'...Upset me?' she shrieked, thumping her fist down on the bed. 'This is what upsets me,' and she tore at the paper, shredding and ripping until the bed was covered in a layer of newsprint. 'My seventeen-year-old daughter had an abortion and I was the last one to know? Did your father know, or Jane, or the next-door neighbours? Did everyone know but me?'

'No, of course not, no one knew, Ma, Please.' I tried to touch her hand but she snatched it away. 'She thought you'd hate her.'

'What sort of a monster did she think I was?'

'It wasn't that. She didn't want to...disappoint you. She loved you, you know that. She wanted you to be proud of her. Oh Ma, please, don't cry, I'm so sorry. I didn't know what to do. I was just a stupid kid.'

But she wasn't listening to my pathetic attempts to excuse myself.

'What sort of a monster did she think I was?' she repeated, then she slammed out of the bedroom and I heard the car start up and accelerate away.

*

When Shon said she'd like to go and stay with some 'friends' in Durban, Ma and Dad went along with it. It was her last year at High School and she said it would be easier to revise for her matrics if she was away from the distractions of life at home. Seemed sensible. Shon had always been the sensible one in our family. I was the one who was always in trouble. I'd lost count of how many detentions I'd done for not wearing school uniform or being late or cheeky or...whatever. My friends were the bad girls, the ones who smoked and skipped off class and had body piercings and tattoos and attitude. Ma was always giving me pep talks about under age, unprotected sex and drugs. But Shon?

'That girl's got her head screwed on the right way, Evie. You grow up like your sister and you won't go far wrong.' There was no need to check up on her because Shon was Shon. However, I wanted to know everything and kept pestering her to tell me about these friends. In the end she got mad with me. 'For Chrissake, Evie, I don't have to tell you everything. Get a life.'

I should have known then that there was something wrong but would it have helped? Maybe not but it doesn't stop me feeling guilty that she had to go through all that horrible stuff on her own. But I was fourteen and bouncing around in my own adolescent hermetically sealed plastic bubble. And I was annoyed

102

with her for keeping secrets and sort of jealous cos she hadn't told me about these new friends. But there were bigger things to worry about in my world, like would the boy I really fancied ever look at me.

She was away for two weeks and Dad and I met her at the bus station when she came back. It was great to see her but she looked wrecked. She said the bus journey had been a nightmare. I nudged her when we were on our way home and Dad was busy cursing the lunatic drivers.

'Too many late nights with the boys? '

She smiled weakly at me and shut her eyes. I took the hint and left her alone. We shared a room so there'd be plenty of time to get all the sordid details later.

Ma was still at work when we got home. If she'd been there she would have given Shon the third degree but she was a nursing sister in the local hospital's A&E department and worked shifts. This week she was on lates and changing to earlies tomorrow. I don't know how she did it but she loved the job.

Shon went straight up to our room for a sleep and she was still flaked out when I took her some dinner later. When I went to bed the plate was still there, food untouched. Shon always slept on her back but this night she was curled up in a ball with the duvet pulled right up to her chin. Her hair was covering her face but when I felt her forehead it was hot and damp. I tried to pull the cover back but she gripped the bedding in her sleep, refusing to let go. I hoped she wasn't ill.

Next morning, when I woke I opened the curtains and bellowed, ' Wakey, wakey', like annoying little sisters do. Shon didn't move so I pulled back the duvet. I must have screamed because her eyes flickered open. She was floating in a sea of red. The blood was orange at the edges and the smell heavy and sickly. I'd never seen so much blood. I turned to run for Ma but Shon managed to grab my arm. Her hands were slippery with sweat.

'No, please. Help me, Evie.'

'Oh my God, Shon, what's happened to you? You're bleeding so much... Please, Ma will know what to do.'

'No!' She dug her nails into my arm. She was shaking her head, half delirious, and her beautiful eyes were full of tears.

I was terrified but somehow I knew this was something you didn't tell your parents about. I cleaned her up as best I could, found a bin bag and put all the bloody sheets and clothes in it, then I sponged down the mattress. She sat on the bedside chair shaking while I found clean pyjamas and bedding. Ma had brought us up to look after ourselves and we had our own laundry cupboard. Now I knew where she was bleeding from I got towels and made them into pads to put beneath her.

'Girls? You getting up?' It was Ma. Shon was terrified so I shot out of the room and met Ma on the landing. She was dressed in her uniform and in a hurry. 'What've you been doing, Evie? It's late.'

'Shon's still asleep. She's got a study day today, so she's gonna have a lie-in and she said she'll see you tonight. But I have to deliver this,' and I gave Ma a huge kiss and twirled her around. 'She can't wait to see you and tell you all the news.' Ma smiled and pushed me away. 'Well keep it down, Evie, if your sister's trying to sleep. Okay, look I'm late, tell lazybones I'm cooking her favourite for tonight. We'll have a lovely family meal together and she can tell us all the news. '

'Great,' I said.

When the house was empty I put Shon's cell in easy reach and told her to ring if she needed me but I don't know if she heard me. She was sleeping again. I stuffed all the bloody sheets and clothes in the washing machine, turned it on, and left for school. I didn't want to leave her but what else could I do? If I didn't turn up at school they'd ring Ma.

That day was the longest of my life. I had to get home and make sure Shon was okay so I bunked out of my last class and ran all the way home. Shon was sitting in a chair by the window when I got to her. She didn't look up when I came in but at least she was out of bed. I knelt beside her and took her hand in mine. 'Are you still bleeding?'

'God will punish me,' she said. 'I'm wicked.'

'No, no you're not....'

'...I took a life, Evie.'

I just kept on stroking her hand. Then I lifted it and kissed it. 'I don't care what you've done, Shon. I'll always love you. Just tell me what to do?'

'Pray for me, baby,' she always called me that. And her voice broke on that 'baby'. When she couldn't cry any more she fell asleep again and I saw to the washing and waited for Ma to come home.

*

The guy was someone Shon hardly knew and didn't much care for. The usual thing – too much to drink and no condom. Ma had brought us up to carry condoms ever since our periods began. It wasn't just unwanted pregnancies she was afraid of, it was Aids. Doesn't matter how much you know, and she'd brought us up knowing everything. We could have run courses on the dangers of unprotected sex. Almost before we could read we knew about birth control, drugs, sexually transmitted diseases, HIV, the lot, but we still do stupid things – all of us.

Dan's Turn

'What was the number of your house, again?' Dan 's voice came from somewhere far away.

I opened my eyes and blinked. We were home. 'There,' I said, 'it's the one with the *For Sale* notice.'

Dan helped me out of the car and we stood side by side on the pavement.

'So, this is where you live?'

'Once upon a time.'

'Looks nice. Evie? You don't hate me do you? For making you tell me about Shon? I didn't want to be cruel.'

'No...It's fine, I'm fine. Look, I'm sorry but I need to get inside. I have to sleep.'

He took my hand and drew me towards him. I staggered a bit and he put his arms around me, steadying me, then, still holding on, he helped me to the front door. I found the key and we went inside.

He must have carried me upstairs because I have no memory of it. I woke up once in the night and saw Dan crouched on the floor beside me. He was texting and the glow from his cell threw shadows on his face, changing his round friendly features into those of a grim-faced stranger.

When I woke again it was daybreak and Dan lay stretched out on the carpet asleep. I went downstairs, drank some water and switched on the telly. There was nothing about V on any of the channels so I switched off and stood in front of the window, watching as the sky filled up with pink-tinged clouds. The weaver birds were already hard at work, flying backwards and forwards to the keerbaum.

'I've got to go away for a few days, Evie.'

Dan was standing in the doorway, his phone in his hand. He was silhouetted against the pink glow of the rising sun and looked like a Ruben's cherub. I almost smiled.

'I'm flying to Belfast, today - Air Emirates.' He came further into the room and stood beside me at the window.

'Belfast?'

'My Da's dying.'

'Your Da?'

'Yeh, he's ill, very ill.'

'You never said.'

'I didn't know till yesterday.'

'I'm sorry.'

'You don't need to be.'

'Of course I do, he's your father.'

'We haven't spoken for years, Evie. But my brother and sister they...they've asked me to go, so...'

'What's the matter with him?'

He shrugged.

'Your father's dying and you don't know what's wrong with him?'

'Oh I know what's wrong with him. Life.'

108

'What?'

'Look, I've got to go.' He put on his coat and slung his backpack over his shoulder.

'But you haven't had any breakfast. I'll make some toast and coffee.'

'I'll get something at the airport.'

'Please, you can't go like this.'

'For God's sake Evie. I don't need anything, I don't want anything.'

'Why are you so angry?'

'Because...because it's just more of the old shit. I thought I'd finished with it a long time ago.'

'I don't understand. Tell me.'

'You're not interested.'

'I am, please, Dan. I want to know.'

He slumped down into the big black chair, dropping his bag on the floor and burying his head in his hands. 'Oh God,' he moaned, scrubbing at his eyes with his fists. 'Here's how it goes. My Da's mother - 'Mammy' they called her - was murdered by the Provisionals when Da was a small child - three years old. She was a widow with six kids. The Provos accused her of being a collaborator and dealt with her accordingly. You think you're the only one who lives in a barbaric country? You don't know the half of it.'

'Was she working for the British? Was she a traitor?'

He shrugged. 'Who knows.'

'What did she do?'

'A young British soldier was shot in the street outside her house and she went out and put a blanket around him and stayed till the medics arrived. So, next day the Provos came for her and Da never saw her again. All these years he's been grieving for his Mammy and now he's dying. All these years hating the British, hating the Provisionals, hating himself, always wanting to find her, to give her a decent burial, writing letters to politicians and political prisoners in The Maze, begging them to tell him where she was.'

'The poor, poor man.'

'Yeah, people felt sorry for him.'

'But not you?'

'God, no. Not me, not any of us kids, except they're more forgiving than me. He was so full of his own pain he never had time for any of us, or our mother. We walked around on tiptoe in that house, frightened to breathe, scared of everyone, especially our father. D'you know what it's like being terrified of the one person who should protect you?' He turned away from me. 'Look I don't want to talk about it. Okay?'

'And your mother?'

"She died years ago. Worn out with all that grief.'

'Did he ever find her - his Mammy?'

'Yeah, finally in the 1990's, when they all *kissed and made up*.

"So, he got her back? That was good.'

'You don't get it do you?' Dan dragged his dead eyes to mine. 'Sure, his Mammy was finally laid to rest in a proper Catholic churchyard with a proper Catholic priest and the Requiem Mass and all, but the Irish mentality is such that no one ever forgives or forgets. There were still some who blamed Mammy for Provo deaths and imprisonments at the time. Da got hate mail. People spat on him as he walked past.'

'But she was innocent?'

'Was she? You see. That's the problem, Evie. What if she was guilty? We'll never know. Never.' He got up and picked up his bag. At the door he stopped and looked at me. 'When Da's in his grave that's it. I'm finished with Ireland. I don't have to be part of it, that's my choice. I can go anywhere in the world, I can be anyone I like. I'm free.'

'But your family?'

'For God's sake, Evie. All my father ever gave me was his bitterness and anger and I tell you, it's not good for the soul. But then you know that, don't you?'

I followed him out to the car and he got in and wound the window down. 'I should get back in a week or so, depending on what happens. There's stuff I have to do while I'm there. You can contact me any time.' He switched on the engine and said something else but I couldn't hear it above the engine noise, so I leant closer. 'I'm not contacting you again, Evie. Okay? If you want me, you know where I am. D'you understand what I'm saying?'

111

I nodded. 'I...I hope it's okay over there, for you. Dan? Are you coming back?'

He stared at me for a moment then he rested his hand gently on the side of my face. 'Stay here, Evie. Keep safe.' And then he was gone.

Back inside I made coffee and checked for messages on my phone but I couldn't concentrate. I tried to imagine the pain Dan's father must have felt, never knowing where his mother was.

*

My sister's funeral took place on a glorious late spring day. The mourners were black cardboard cut-outs against a Walt Disney blue sky and the fynbos was a kaleidoscope of blowsy gaudiness. It was the sort of day that took your breath away.

I remember Ben asking, '*Why is my Auntie Shon behind bars?*' when he saw the metal trellis around the coffin. And Jane, sobbing as if she'd never stop. And Ma standing there so calm and serene and saying all those lovely, heart-breaking things about Shon. And little Mandy taking her grandad's hand the next morning and saying. '*Hurry, eat your breakfast, we have to go get my Auntie Shon now.*'

The black thing was the one job Ma entrusted to me. I was supposed to let everyone know not to wear black but I couldn't even get that right. So, it was only Ma and me in bright colours. I wore red and Ma was in a dress with flowers cascading down the bodice in all the colours of the rainbow. She wore a hat too, that one I'd dreamt about. Some ridiculous creation that Shon and I had made her buy that day. I don't know why Shon wanted Ma to wear a hat. I couldn't give a toss whether she wore one or not. I didn't even want to go to my graduation. Dressing up in one of those stupid gowns and wearing a ridiculous mortarboard and for what? For a third class degree in a mickey-mouse subject? I'd overheard my dear father calling it that and he was right. But Shon was adamant and in the end she always got her way. I think she probably had a lot of our father's genes in her, like little sister Jane. Ma and I were more alike but she was much nicer than me. So Ma ended up with a hat - not a fascinator. It was red and wide-brimmed and she wore it on the side of her head like one of those 1940's gangster-moll movie stars, like Marlene Dietrich. She looked great in it.

After the funeral I waited until they'd all gone back to the cars, then I stood at the edge of the grave and threw my bunch of wild flowers high into the air. I watched as the petals pattered down on the coffin. 'I love you, Shon, I always will. I'm going to find him, however long it takes. He's not going to get away with it. I promise.' I said the words to the sky, because that's where she was, not in that hole in the ground.

Ma

After Dan went I spent the rest of that day drifting around the house. He had made me uneasy and unsure of what I should do next. I needed to keep strong and focused. I don't know what I was looking for in the rooms, but whatever it was I didn't find it. I'd tried coming back once before but it hadn't worked then either. People said that in time I would be able to remember Shon and Ma as they were, before any of this happened, but it doesn't work like that for me. All it did was fill my mind with the things I desperately needed to forget.

*

After Shon's death I got compassionate leave from work and moved back into the family home to 'help'. Not much help. Ma took charge. At that time she was amazing. She cooked huge meals for us that no one ate. People came to offer their sympathy and support and they'd go away clutching casseroles and cakes. The phone rang incessantly, cards poured through the door - why? Was it someone's birthday? The undertakers came, the local pastor called and Ma chose Shon's favourite hymns. She wrote and read the eulogy. She even picked out the clothes that Shon would 'wear' at her funeral. She must have seen my look of horror when she came down with an armful of clothes and asked me which I thought Shon would have liked. *'Well, we couldn't let them bury her in one of those awful taffeta frilly things could we?'*

A few weeks after the funeral she went back to work, part-time. She was so incredibly calm and together, The rest of us were like zombies and when she wasn't looking we watched her fearfully, waiting for the storm to break.

I can't remember exactly when it all went wrong but one night I was woken from a deep alcohol-induced sleep by a rhythmic thudding sound, coming from downstairs. My bedroom was over the kitchen. At first I thought it was burglars but when I listened carefully I recognised the sound - someone was ironing. It was 4 a.m. and pitch black. I dragged myself out of bed and padded down to the kitchen.

When I opened the door I found Ma bent over the ironing board. She didn't look up and when I spoke she ignored me and continued ironing, as if her life depended on it. I went back to bed.

*

She used to say, '*Ironing is the only chore I enjoy. I love getting the creases out of things and making them smooth and perfect.*' She even ironed our school socks. As a child I remember waking up to the rocking sound of the ironing board. It was as comforting then as a lullaby. It meant I could snuggle down for half an hour before I had to get up for school. When I finally dragged myself down into the kitchen, still half asleep, Ma would look up and smile and the early morning sun would be on her face and the tendrils of damp hair blowing across her mouth, which she blew away. The smell of clean linen and freshly made toast was like an early morning blessing.

*

115

That first day set the pattern and every morning from then on, there she'd be, ironing. When she was done she would go back to. bed and stay there, all day, sometimes. I got to hate the sound of that ironing. I wore headphones and turned the volume to max but I still heard that *thud-thudding*.

If there was nothing to iron she took the curtains down and ironed them. She staggered downstairs with drawer-loads of clean clothes from all the rooms, and ironed everything again. She washed and ironed all the things Shon had left hanging in wardrobes when she moved into her own place.

She gave up her job and stopped talking to us. It was as if a switch had been turned off in her brain. We knew that something had to break in Ma. She couldn't go on behaving in the same way. I suppose I was a bit relieved at first, because this behaviour seemed like 'normal' grieving. Anyway, that's what the doc said. She needed to have a little breakdown before she could begin to come to terms with what had happened. Yes that's what he said, a kindly man, we'd known him all our lives, but *'come to terms with'* her daughter's rape and murder? Seriously?

Ma never got dressed again. She spent her days walking the house in an old once-pink dressing gown.

Mary had worked for Ma since she was a young child and she became Ma's carer. Dad was back at work and it was time for me to go back too, I didn't want to lose my job. I commuted from home.

Dad never commented on what was going on. He and Ma weren't sleeping together anymore. They hadn't been for a long time. I often found the settee with a duvet slung over it and empty cups and newspapers strewn all over the floor in the morning. Dad and I didn't talk much. I never mentioned the ironing thing to him. He went off to work the same as usual, came home late, ate, watched telly. The only bright spot for Dad was when Jane visited with her two, and he would build Lego with Ben, and read to Mandy.

I wrote lists. Things Shon said she wanted to do with her life, places she wanted to visit and people she liked and music and films she loved...and how many babies she wanted. I scribbled it all down randomly and when I went to read it back the next day I often couldn't read what I'd written. I don't know why I didn't use my tablet. All I knew was it felt right to write longhand. It made it real. I had to get it all down before I forgot.

I told her things too, like my secrets and how much I loved her and missed her. I owned up to the mean things I'd done to her that she never knew about, like when I'd used her sandals to make foot-prints in the soil to hide mine when I'd raided Dad's strawberry patch. She got two punishments-one for being greedy and one for being a liar. Sorry Shon. And the time I hadn't passed on the phone message from Roddy something - the most gorgeous kif boy in our street - so that he thought she didn't want to go out with him. My hand ached from all that writing.

117

One Tuesday night I was late getting back from work. Tuesdays were Mary's day off. We didn't like leaving Ma on her own for too long so I was panicking a bit. Jane tried to pop in when she could but she had the kids to ferry about to school and stuff. There'd been an editorial meeting at work and Frankie had made it clear that I should be there if I wanted to keep my job. They had been very understanding in the aftermath of Shon's death but enough was enough.

The frenzied woman who'd been inhabiting the body of my mother had left the house for good now, but another, more frightening one, had taken up residence - a suspicious, nasty one. It was about seven o'clock and nearly dark when I got home. There were no lights on and I hurried inside calling *'Ma,'* as I shut the door. I hated the dark now and I switched on all the lights. *'Ma? Where are you?'* I found her sitting in her chair in the kitchen. She was so still I thought she must be asleep but her eyes were wide open, staring.

'D'you want a coffee, Ma?'

At the sound of my voice she turned to look at me. 'Did you see her today, Evie?' I was so pleased that she'd remembered my name.

I sat down in the chair opposite and took off my shoes. 'Who, Ma?'

She glanced at me and sighed heavily. 'You're always like this. You like playing games don't you? You, and that other one.'

'What other one, Ma?' She was frightening me now. 'I don't know who you mean.'

She sat forward in her chair and I thought she wanted to whisper something in my ear so I leant towards her. The full weight of her fist caught me on the side of my face and sent me sprawling. When I scrambled to my feet, clutching my jaw, she was staring at me, as if she'd never seen me before.

When Dad came in I was in my bedroom in hysterics. That was the night he must have decided to leave because later that week he didn't come home. He texted me a list of things he wanted and arranged for a removal man to collect them one evening. I had no idea where he was going to live, or with whom. He moved out while Ma was still alive. I don't think she noticed, but I did and I'll never speak to him again. Jane made excuses for him as usual.

My parent's marriage had been dodgy for years but after Shon's death it didn't stand a chance. Shon and I had always known that Dad was a serial womaniser and their relationship was screwed, but for some reason they stuck together. Knowing Ma it was probably for our sake. She wanted us to have a stable family life. Jane refused to say or think anything bad about our father. She worshipped him and she was his good little daughter, ran around after him wanting to please him. Ironic that because she didn't run around after her own husband, Lee. Maybe there's only room for one man in your life.

119

Ma died six months after Shon. She took an overdose. I thought afterwards that maybe that's why she went back to work. She'd planned it all along? Free access to the drug's cabinet. *Roll up, roll up, get your death medication here.* She took the pills, lay down on Shon's bed and died. She didn't leave a farewell note but we didn't need one. We knew she blamed herself for her daughter's death and thought that if she'd been a better mother it would never have happened. That's shit but that's what she believed. She'd devoted too much time to her job and not enough to us three. She should have visited Shon more often. She had her doubts about Nick Ground from the start but she thought it wasn't her business. She'd brought us up to learn from our mistakes. That's how we mature, she said, but then Shon died and all that Ma believed in crumbled like so much dried-up dung.

I wasn't surprised by her suicide, just at how long it had taken her to do it. Part of me was envious. She was with Shon. I wasn't religious but I knew they were together - absolutely knew it.

It was me who found Ma. There was a photo in her hand - it was one of her and Shon - but Ma's head had been cut off. Shon was about twelve, by the look of her, a beautiful child with long brown limbs. She was laughing and looking up at where Ma should have been, as if they were sharing some huge joke. I could see Ma's arm around her waist, as if she was tickling her.

The Plan

It's ten days now, since Dan left. I haven't contacted him. What would I say? I've spent the days going over and over the plan. I've covered every smallest detail and now all that's left is to be patient and vigilant. I can feel it all building up like one of those tsunami waves. The birds have stopped singing.

The tweets and retweets and comments and likes have been pouring in from Melanie and her uncle, and even her brother.

'V wants to say thank you, E, for your support - we all call him V now. We like your V for Victory.'

'Prison is hard. V has even cried on occasion. I wanted so much to hug him but no physical contact is allowed.'

'God bless the poor suffering soul. I reply. *He is constantly in my prayers.'*

'V is battling with prison.'

I say. *'God give him the strength to survive this ordeal.'*

Terry Davey died today. It was a miracle he'd survived this long. Shame he didn't live long enough to see his daughter's butcher punished properly but at least he doesn't have to worry now. It's Thea I'm sorry for. I wished I could share my plan with her. I think she would have appreciated it. Maybe, we could have become friends. I tweeted her as E, telling her I was totally impressed with her courage and loyalty to her uncle and passing on my deepest condolences. She didn't reply. I didn't expect her to. My message felt as insincere as the ones I send to the Heineys. That's what flat words do, they sink into oblivion like ink on blotting paper. You can put as many lol's and :D's and :)'s and :('s you want, but you can't convey any true feeling.

Thea had visited her uncle daily since the accident, reading to him, playing his music, holding his hand, singing his favourite songs. YouTube even had a compilation of the tunes, so that people can download them. Does that sound sick to you or is it just me? If Terry Davey blinked we all knew about it within hours. This is the age of communication after all. Thea never said much when interviewed except one day when some stupid interviewer asked her if she was glad there was 'closure' now, so that her family could get on with their lives. She looked at the interviewer as if he was mad. *"Closure?" What closure?'* and then, after a moment, *'and what 'family?'*

The last day or two I've been reading a lot. Ma had a huge collection of gardening books. So much information. I find a page I'm interested in and leave the book open in whichever room I happen to be in. There are books all over the place. When my eyes ache too much I make truffles and send them to Melanie. She seems to like them, or perhaps she's just being kind. I imagine the clan opening yet another box of sweets and going, 'What's that crazy bitch done now?'

I eat ready-meals - plastic pap - I'm not hungry but I know I have to eat. I stay out of the house for most of the day. I walk the streets and the parks. If it's raining I go into a cafe and make a latte last a very long time. I don't want to be in the house if prospective buyers come. I saw a bakkie outside one day on my way home, so I walked past my gate and waited around the corner till I knew the coast was clear.

I am invisible. There is no trace of me when I go out, except the chocolate and cream and milk in the fridge. I put the books in neat piles. Once or twice someone, probably Jane, brings fresh flowers to 'dress' the house and plug in the air fresheners again. I wonder who she thinks is unplugging them? Maybe they've got a cleaner coming in too, although I've seen no one. The gardener hasn't been again. Not since that first morning. There's no one to spy on me now because the house next door, that used to have nosey neighbours, is up for sale. Maybe our house leaches its sadness everywhere. You can feel it. I quite like it - like the idea that bricks and mortar can grieve too. Maybe I really am going mad.

I get a daily text from Jane. *'Where are you, woman?' 'We need to talk.'* Always hectoring, always expecting some reaction. Well, I'm past 'reactions'. I'm on that single path again, that single thought.

But the memories get jealous, they don't like being ignored, and sometimes they creep up on me while I'm not looking.

*

After Ma's death I went back to my Wendy house in Cape Town and started work. For the first few weeks Frankie gave me copy editing to do from home. A kid I'd never seen before used to deliver the work. He was a young, beautiful boy, just out of High

School, resentful of this menial task, never looking me in the eye. He used to shove the envelope at me then disappear without a word. His indifference suited me. No one cared about me, me least of all. The sooner it was over the better. I just wanted to lie down, close my eyes and never wake up. I used to walk across busy streets without looking. I didn't eat properly and I drove like a maniac until the day I nearly knocked down a little kid. I got rid of my car after that and bought an old bike off my landlord.

When I returned to the newsroom the Viktor Heiney murder trial was big news. I followed every detail of the case and became an expert on the law of dolus eventualis. And out of all this concentrated studying I began to see that life was worth living after all, because now I had a purpose. I felt the best I'd felt since Shon's death. I even rang Jane and told her I was back at work. Don't know why I did that but I soon regretted it because she obviously thought it was her nagging or 'counselling', as she liked to call it, that had made me see sense. I didn't disabuse her because it suited my purposes for her to believe it was down to her.

I even convinced myself that there was a chance that she and I might have some sort of relationship. She was my sister after all and Shon and Ma had loved her kids. We should try to get along for their sakes. We met up for coffee a few times. She told me Dad was living with a woman in Hermanus. I managed not to say anything but she saw my expression. 'It wasn't all his fault, you know, Evie.' she said, 'Ma wasn't perfect.' Yeah, well that's when that particular conversation came to an abrupt end.

She rang me a few days later to ask me to dinner. She said the kids would love to see their auntie. I said *yes*. I'd just been to V's bail hearing and felt quite upbeat. I considered making Jane a cushion too. I had a lot of material left. The meal was okay, Jane's husband Lee's a nice guy and the kids were fun. While Lee put them to bed Jane and I finished off the wine. Without thinking I started to talk about the court case and how surprised I was that Heiney had got bail when he was obviously guilty as hell.

Jane was quiet for a moment, then she put down her glass and said in her best, talking-down voice to a very small - very stupid - child. 'We all know he did it, Evie. He admits it, that's not what this trial is about. The point is whether he did it on purpose? What if he really is innocent? What if it really was a tragic mistake?'

I shook my head, closed my eyes and took a deep breath. 'He shot her at point blank range three times, Jane. Some mistake.'

But Jane always had an answer. 'Just because Shon was murdered by her boyfriend doesn't mean that Viktor Heiney's guilty of murder too, does it?'

I was too shocked to speak. The witch. What was she doing living in my head?

But she hadn't finished. 'You might think I'm stupid, Evie, but I know what you're like. You've been walking around in a dream for months and now, suddenly you're back at work, acting normally. Look...' and she lowered her voice and smiled at me. I expected her to pat me on the head. '...This thing with Shon? You've got to let it go. It's...unhealthy, Evie. Shon wouldn't have wanted you to be like this.'

'It's got nothing to do with Shon, you stupid cow...' I yelled.

...'Really?' she said, refusing to be angry. 'So? Why are you so interested in the trial then? You're not really covering it for the paper are you? You're on holiday, at least that's what they told me, when I tried to ring you the other day. So what's it all about? Is this the behaviour of a rational human being?'

I didn't reply but that didn't deter my sister. She could carry on a two-way discussion on her own, no problem.

'It happened, Evie, and yes it was terrible, but there's nothing you or I or anyone can do about it. Nick Ground is never going to be caught. It's heart-breaking, but it's true. If you want to do something for Shon and Ma then live your life. Don't let him win. He's already killed our sister, don't let the bastard kill you too. You've got to forget about Viktor Heiney. He's not Nick Ground.'

'I know that. D'you think I'm crazy?'

She shrugged and looked away.

'I want to see justice done. Is that too much to ask? He has to pay for what he's done.'

'But that's the whole point, Evie, what has he done? '

I got up and marched to the door.

'That's right,' she jeered. 'Run away. And you're the one so keen on the truth.'

I turned to face her and shook my head slowly. 'You believe that...creep...that murdering bastard?'

'Think about the evidence. The night Rachel Davey was killed he was recovering from a serious knee injury. He was on a morphine derivative pain killer. He testified that he'd been shocked awake by a particularly gruesome drug-induced dream and saw a figure in the darkened doorway. He thought it was a nightmare intruder coming to kill him and his girlfriend, so in his psychotic panic he grabbed his gun and fired.'

'What lunatic keeps a loaded gun beside his bed, for God's sake?'

'Exactly my point, Evie. For that instant he was a *lunatic*, a madman, someone who wasn't responsible for his actions.' She was quiet for a moment. 'I know you're not going to thank me for saying this but have you thought about seeing a shrink? Dad and I think it might help.'

Jane

Jane didn't know I was staying in the house until tonight. I was reading upstairs when I heard the front door open. I wasn't scared. What was the worst thing that could happen? Dying wasn't a scary thought for me, the alternative was much worse.

It was getting dark and Jane screeched when she saw me coming towards her down the stairs in the half-light. She switched on the lights and stood there, swinging her bag around her head, ready to defend herself. My sister had guts if nothing else. When she recognised me she was furious.

After she'd stopped yelling I put the kettle on. She lectured me while it boiled. 'Why didn't you let me know you were staying here? You could have saved me the trouble of coming round all the time to check that everything's okay. And anyway, why are you here?'

If I'm honest I actually like Jane. She gives me a reason to stay angry. 'It's my home, why shouldn't I be here?'

'What's happened to your place in Cape Town and your job? Don't tell me. You've got the push haven't you? Yeah, that's it, isn't it? Well I can't say I'm surprised, the way you've been carrying on. I'm only surprised it lasted this long.'

I thumped her coffee down in front of her and walked out of the kitchen. She followed.

'It's sold, you know - the house. We're just waiting to exchange contracts. So, you'll have to get out soon. The power is being switched off tomorrow.'

'Can I come live with you, Janey?'

She ignored my pathetic attempt at humour.

'So? What happened?'

I shrug. 'Money ran out. When do we get our cut of this place?'

'Soon as the cheque clears. Look, Evie, I could lend you some rand if you're skint. Lee and I have a bit put by.'

The thought of being in Jane's debt appalled me. 'That won't be necessary. Tell Dad to text me when the money's in my bank account. '

'Don't you want to see him to thank him, in person?'

I raise my eyebrows at her.

'He didn't have to split it with us, Evie. By rights he could have kept the lot.'

'More fool him then.'

'Evie, when's this...stupid vendetta between you and Dad going to end?'

'When he's dead, or I am.'

'What's he ever done to you to make you hate him so much?'

'Nothing. He's never done anything to me, or for me, or encouraged me, or loved me...'

'...Oh, God, here we go again. The lament of Evie Adze'.

Jane could win prizes with her exasperated sigh. But then she said something that truly stopped me in my tracks,

'At least Mary must be glad you're here. God knows why, but she always had a soft spot for you.'

'Mary?'

'Yes, Mary. Remember her? About fifty, bit of a limp, worked for us all our lives. Got her?'

'Of course I remember Mary. But why would she be glad I'm here?'

Jane had that smile on her face that I always wanted to rip off. 'Well, you're neighbours, aren't you? Yeah, strange old world isn't it? I wonder who would have looked after Mary if Dad hadn't? Would it be our Evie?' She shook her head. 'No, not Evie. Because she is too busy feeling sorry for herself. Don't you ever think that Dad and I might be suffering too? Of course not. We don't make a fuss or spend every living moment walking about with tragic faces like you. I bet you never even gave Mary a thought and she was Ma's closest friend for all those years, her only friend at the end.'

'Mary's living here? In the shed?'

'Yeah. Just down the garden. You must have seen her.' She saw my face and clapped her hands together in delight. 'God. That's priceless. How d'you do it? You live on a different planet to everyone else. Unbelievable.'

So, it had been Mary I saw that first day. "Is she here now?'

Jane shook her head. 'She only stays when she's doing the garden, and, seeing as you're so interested, Dad's arranged for her to move into an annexe at their house. So you don't have to worry about her anymore, which is lucky because you haven't been, have you?'

'So what does his fancy woman think about that?'

'Fancy woman?' And there I was thinking you were the 'seen it all', 'done it all', hard-nosed journalist', not some prissy little prude. Vanessa, yeah that's her name, is a nice woman. She's great with my kids. It almost makes up for them losing their grandma and aunties.' She let that thought hang in the air for a moment. 'And, she's good for Dad. He and Ma should never have married. It was a shotgun wedding after all - oh sorry, didn't you know that? So? D'you want anything? From the house? A reminder? It's your last chance. I'm taking what I want tonight.'

'Are you going soon?'

'When I'm ready.' She paused for a moment. 'Of course...it was you who's been pulling out the air freshener's. I might have guessed. And is that your chocolate and cream in the fridge?'

'Yeh.'

'I didn't want to see it go to waste.'

I watched the telly while she marched in and out with piles of useless tat. It's the news and I'm trying to concentrate. They're giving details about Terry Davey's death and there are shots of a distraught Thea coming out of the hospital. There's a close up of her lashing out at a photographer as she's pushed and shoved. No sign of Magda or the Needals. Maybe they're too ashamed to show their faces. I'm about to switch off when there's another news flash. I can feel my heart beating really fast. A reporter says V has been seriously injured in a prison attack and is being transferred to the trauma unit in Cape Town's Central hospital.

'Bet you're glad.' Jane says from the doorway. 'They thought someone would get him when he was inside. They're animals in there.'

I squat in front of the telly with my fingers in my ears. V is being stretchered into an ambulance surrounded by police and journalists. He's cuffed and there's a shot of his white, shocked face. After the report there's an interview with some legal guy who thinks V will spend the rest of his sentence in an open prison, if he survives. I sit back on my heels and stare at the screen. I don't know how to react. If he dies then...then what? I don't want him dead and a victim. I thumped my fists down on the floor.

Jane stalked off and I went back to the chair and sank down, closing my eyes. I willed her to go, so that I could think. What would I do if V died? Would that be the end? After a few minutes Jane came back in with a photo album and dropped it in my lap. 'Have a look.'

Ma loved photos and used to write comments underneath like *Evie in a bad mood*, or *Evie in another bad mood,* and so on. It had been funny back then. My ipad attempts at photography made her laugh. *'How can you take proper pictures with that baking tray? You should get a proper camera.'*

I flicked through the pages of the album and found one of me and Shon on the beach at Noordhoek. We were holding conch shells against our ears. I remember that day. Shon used to have

132

this dream about drowning, but it wasn't horrible, she said, because she was a mermaid and she would drift down through the water and see all the beautiful sea creatures and coloured seaweeds and coral and shining abalone shells. She said mermaids talked to her when she put a shell to her ear and I was jealous because I never heard the mermaids.

Jane came in and saw what I was looking at and laughed. 'You always had a pop belly when you were a kid didn't you? '

I slammed the album shut.

'Are you sure you don't want to take anything? This is our last chance.' I shook my head. She picked up the album and leafed through. 'There're some classic ones of you.'

She left the album with me and made a final tour of the house. I heard her opening and shutting cupboards and drawers. I wanted to have the photo of me and Shon with the shells, but before I got to it I turned over a page and there was a space where someone had removed a picture. The caption was still there. *'Shon and Ma sharing a joke.'*

I'd got the fire going nicely by the time Jane was ready to leave. 'God,' she complained poking her head around the door. 'What d'you need that for? 'It's like a bloody furnace in here.' But then she saw what I was doing. I'd ripped all the photographs out of the album and was burning them, one by one in the grate. I expected her to scream at me but she didn't, she just stood there watching our childhood going up in flames.

To V from E

I got a tweet from Melanie after Jane left. I can't believe it. She's asked me to come to the hospital tomorrow. V's on life support. All the family and friends will be there, keeping vigil. Would I join them? Would I!

One more night and I'm out of here. I've got enough money for a cheap room in Cape Town while I wait for the house money to come through. Don't know what'll happen after that. Suddenly I'm full of energy. Jane was right, we had been happy in this house, once. She had found so many things she wanted to keep but she was that sort of person. She still had school friends going back to the year dot. I hadn't kept in touch with anyone, ever. One thing Jane was wrong about though, there was something I wanted to take with me.

It was a beautiful moonlit night and I collected everything I needed before going out into the back garden. I tied a scarf over my nose and mouth.

'Tread carefully, Evie. Look out for puff adders.' It was Ma's voice and then Shon's laugh. *'They wouldn't dare bite our Evie, Ma. She tastes nasty.'*

'No I don't, you do,' I shouted, my voice loud in the stillness.

Shining the torch at my feet I walked carefully across the grass to the path that ran down the length of the garden. The grass was cut but everything else was overgrown and wild. I passed a frangipani with its delicate star-like flowers and on past the keerbaum, festooned with cascading pink blossoms that glinted like wax in the moonlight. A boomslang used to live in this tree - a small green pretty little snake, with a dainty triangular head and enough venom to kill an elephant. But the fangs pointed backwards, so when the snake caught a small rodent or fledgling it would swallow the prey before the venom was injected. If you wanted to be bitten you would have to stick your finger right down the snake's throat.

I forced my way down the path that opened out beside Mary's shed. It was incredible that she'd been here all this time and we hadn't met. If I got enough money from Dad I'd give some to her. A delicate sweet scent was drifting towards me on the warm night air and I swept the torch up ahead of me to where an insignificant little tree grew. It was covered in a froth of whitey-pink flowers - Acokanthera oppositifolia - Ma's pride and joy. Pulling on some gardening gloves I chipped off some of the bark and dropped it in a canvas bag, then I took it back to the old tree stump outside our backdoor and hammered the pieces of wood. I put the powdered wood and bits of bark in a big old potjie pot and filled it to the brim with water. There was kindling in the fire-pit and I heaved the pot on top, gave it a stir, and lit the fire. Shining the torch on my cell, I saw it was 8 p.m. - twelve hours before it was done. I had to check it through the night to make sure the water didn't evaporate before the time was up. When the water began to bubble gently I put the lid on and weighted it down with several bricks to stop animals tipping it over in the night. I made myself comfortable on a chair outside the kitchen door. There were some old blankets in the cupboard under the stairs. The moon and stars were so bright I didn't need the kitchen light on. The darkness was warm and comforting. I felt so at peace. It was all coming to an end.

In the morning I pulled up the scarf again and looked inside the pot. The water had completely evaporated and there was a thick, black, sticky residue in the bottom of the pot. Putting my gloves back on I went in search of a red euphorbia that grew against the garden fence. Snipping off some stems I took them back to the pot and held them over the black substance so that the plant's sap oozed into the mixture and I stirred until it became a sticky glue. I carried the pot to the back door to cool. There were traces of sap on my gloves and I peeled them off carefully and put them into a rubbish bag. I put the bricks into the bag too.

Back inside I melted the chocolate in a pan. It was important to work quickly because I couldn't chance the electricity going off before I'd finished. When the truffle mixture was ready I added the black glue and some Southern Comfort to make the right consistency. Finally, I rolled the truffles in finely- chopped pistachios and placed them in gold sweet cases. I selected the best ten and threw the extras in the rubbish bag. The sweets looked so pretty in the heart-shaped box. There were some gift bags under the sink and I placed the box inside one, with a card. *To V from E.*

After I'd washed my hands and the cooking utensils thoroughly, I started on the house. There was a lot to be done - scrubbing and washing - every trace of me to be got rid of and the house left spotless. I was in the kitchen wiping down the surfaces when I heard a noise outside and thought it might be some animal nosing around the pot. I flung open the door, prepared to chase whatever it was, but came face to face with Mary. She was standing there staring at me.

'My God, Mary, where did you spring from?'

Her expression was blank.

My heart was racing but I had to stay calm. 'Don't just stand there, come in. I have to leave soon but we've time for some tea. I think there's some rooibos somewhere.'

She didn't move. I took a step towards her, holding out my hand, but she backed away.

'Mary, what's the matter? Don't you know me? It's me, Evie.'

She put her hand to her mouth and looked at the open potjie pot and then back at me. 'What have you done, Evie?'

'Nothing. I don't know what you mean.'

'Don't lie to me. You made this...' and she jabbed her finger at the pot. 'You made this poison?'

'It's fine. It's nothing, I was just...experimenting. Seeing how to make it.'

'Why? Why would you want to see " how to make it". This isn't a child's game, Evie. This is poison. Very bad poison.'

'I can explain.'

'Explain? You want to explain to me? I am a San, I know about Bushman's poison. My grandfather used it to bring food for his family. You? What do you want this bad thing for?'

'Nothing, I ...'

'...It's wrong, Evie. There are evil, bad people in our world but God will punish them, not you or me. It is not our job. Ma would not like it.'

'Come inside, please, we need to talk.'

'No, I will not come into this house again. I live with Mr Adze. This house belongs to someone else. A stranger.'

'But I want you to understand, Mary. Please, listen to me.'

But she shook her head and hurried away. I didn't follow her; what would have been the point? She'd been brutalised by her husband for years, surely she must understood about justice? But I couldn't think about her, not now. I mustn't.

I heaved the potjie pot under the outside tap and let the water run until it ran clear and then I emptied the water and filled the pot with earth and pushed it deep into the bushes.

On the way to the station I took a shortcut through the park and waited on the bridge until there was no one around. Then I dropped the weighted rubbish sack into the deepest part of the ornamental lake. It sank immediately.

The station cafe was full of families and groups of teenagers waiting to get to Cape Town. Many of them were in party clothes, wearing face paint and garish wigs. It took me a moment to remember what this day was. It was the Mardi Gras, the Cape Town carnival - a huge extravaganza with thousands of musicians, singers and dancers. Elaborate floats and jazz bands paraded the streets and the carnival ended in a huge all-night street party. Shon and I had loved it. It was a celebration of the city's diversity and racial integration and a time to forget all that was wrong with the country. One year Shon was in a dance group. She wore this sexy silver space suit and carried a space gun filled with bubbles that she 'shot' the little kids with. We partied all that night. It was before Nick Ground, when Shon and I were happy.

I sat in a corner, trying to block out all the noise and joy. The cafe was one of those places that had TV screens everywhere you looked. A leading ANC politician was being interviewed for CNN. The female interviewer was giving the man a hard time. She pointed out that the Heiney case had triggered protests world-wide and Zuma was in a corner. He must be forced to address domestic violence and rape issues in South Africa. She questioned the validity of passing off domestic violence as the prerogative of the poor and disenfranchised, or that, within tribal South Africa, wife beating could ever be condoned. Men and women were demanding justice for every woman who suffered at the hands of their partners, be they rich or poor, black or white.

The Carnival

Melanie had asked me to be at the hospital after 2 pm so, when I got to Cape Town, I had time to kill. I bought a *Chronicle* and sat on a bench, flicking through the pages, while sightseers surged past. The carnival proper didn't start until nightfall but there were funfairs and entertainments dotted all over the city.

Who's Sorry Now? ran the headline in the paper, with a full page shot of V being transferred to an ambulance outside the prison. The report was written by Dan Kinelly. So? He was back.

When it was time to leave I found the press bracelet I'd pinched in my backpack, and slipped it on my wrist. It might come in useful at the hospital. After this I went into the Ladies and washed my face, cleaned my teeth, combed my hair and changed into a clean T-shirt I looked almost presentable by the time I came out and headed for the left luggage area where I stowed my back-pack in a locker. All I had to carry was the gift bag.

When I joined the people, spilling out of the station and onto the pavements, it was incredibly hot, and I wished I'd worn something cooler. I worried that the chocolate might melt and I didn't want to meet Melanie stinking of sweat. It would take twenty minutes to walk to the unit and I mustn't arrive early, so I ambled along keeping to the shallow waters at the edge of the torrent of people.

No one looked at me. I was alone and scared again, like that first morning in big school when I didn't know anyone and that girl looked at me in a scary way, like she was marking me

140

down to eat later, and I wet myself, because I was too frightened to put my hand up to be excused. The teacher let Shon take me home to get changed. 'Don't worry,' she said, squeezing my hand, on the way back to school. 'Every kid pees in their pants the first day. It's an initiation, and you passed.' Then she laughed and I did too, because I could be brave with my sister beside me.

As I stumbled along I made myself concentrate on what I would do afterwards. I hadn't considered 'afterwards' until now. Maybe I should pay someone to deliver the truffles for me? That way they wouldn't know it was me. But did I want to get away with it? I hadn't cared before but now...and if I paid some guy, what if he didn't deliver it or he wasn't allowed inside the hospital and took the sweets home for his kids? I wasn't even sure how long it would take for the poison to work. I should have done more research on quantities per body weight. And what if he didn't die? And what if I was wrong?

That thought stopped me dead in my tracks and the woman behind thumped into my back. She stared belligerently at me before marching away, Suddenly it was all too much. I couldn't do it. I looked frantically around for an escape route but something was happening up ahead. The crowds were thinning. There was an intersection and the mass of people were turning left towards the sea, leaving the way ahead clear. I kept on putting one foot in front of the other and suddenly there it was, the hospital, straight ahead of me and it was exactly 2 o'clock.

At first I thought I must have come to the wrong place. I had expected a media frenzy but it looked so normal. I watched as ambulances came and went and visitors and patients entered and exited the main entrance. The only hint that something unusual was happening was an orderly queue of people waiting to get inside the hospital through a small side-entrance. There were some newsmen milling about but everyone was quiet and respectful. Was he dead? I couldn't think about that, I had to get inside and see Melanie. Hospital security staff were checking people as they went into the building so I joined the queue. There was a group of Heiney supporters from the trial in front of me and I tagged along behind them. One of the women glanced at me and smiled and the guard let me in with them.

There was the same feeling of calm inside the building. A group of people stood to one side, in a roped-off area. They were in a circle holding hands and softly singing hymns. I saw V's brother with the uncle and other family members and friends but Melanie wasn't with them. I looked around the room for her. There was a large media presence, just standing about, as if waiting for the main event to begin. I saw Frankie talking to a colleague and beside her was Dan. He was looking straight at me. I couldn't read his expression but I looked away. I can't explain what it did to me, seeing him like that.

A hand touched my arm.

It was Melanie. 'I knew it was you,' she whispered, drawing me close and hugging me. 'Thank you, E. Thank you so much for being here.'

I was surprised. 'It's my pleasure, but how did you know?'

She smiled. 'What? How did I know you were E?' She had such a warm smile. 'Who else could it have been? My brother and I had a bet on it. I've won.' She waved towards the group and I saw her brother wave back. 'It was easy. There weren't that many supporters for V on your side of the courtroom. In fact you were the only one.'

She laughed at my confusion, then she lifted my hand and kissed it. 'I'll never forget your kindness, none of us will - especially V.'

I wanted to hate her, to see ugliness in her, but she had such a nice face, very like her brother, delicately boned with lovely black hair. She was a beautiful woman, but not today, not for some time. Her skin was yellowish and puffy and her eyes were set in dark circles. She looked as if she'd been born crying. Whatever her brother had done she didn't deserve this.

'How is he?'

She took a shuddering breath, then wiped her tears with the back of her hand. 'He's...broken. They did terrible things to him...but there's always hope isn't there? Come and join us,' she said, pulling me towards her family and friends and their singing. But I couldn't sing hymns with them, I just couldn't, so I held up the gift bag, like an offering, to distract her. 'Can I give these to V?'

She shook her head. 'No, I'm sorry, he's being fed intravenously. It's such a pity because I know how much it would have meant to him to see you. But maybe another day?'

I nodded. 'Yes, another day.' I had to get out of there. 'I'm glad I've met you, Melanie.'

'Are you going so soon?'

'Sorry, but I must. Things to do, you know?'

'Well, if you must.'

I turned to go but she rested a hand on my shoulder, stopping me.

'You could leave the truffles with me if you like. I could give them to him when he's better? ' She held out her hand.

This was all going wrong. She saw my hesitation.

'I want him to see them, E, even if he can't eat them. It will mean so much to him.' And she took the bag out of my hands.

'No,' I said, trying not to panic. I had to be certain that V ate the truffles - no one else. 'They'll go stale, Melanie. I use fresh ingredients. I can easily make him some more when he's better. Please, let me have them.'

But she wasn't listening. '... and you made that beautiful cushion for him and sent all those kind messages. People like you have kept us sane.' She patted her tummy. 'Though I have you to blame for all this extra weight.'

She was heroic, making jokes to make me feel better. I thrust out my hand. 'No, please. I'll make V something spectacular when he's well.'

But she lifted the box high in the air, out of my reach. 'It's okay. We can eat them if V can't, although I have to ration my little brother. or he'd eat the lot.'

I was frantic now. 'You can't. I'd feel dreadful if they weren't...perfect.' I made a lunge at them and, as I did so, the sleeve of my shirt rolled down exposing my arm. I heard Melanie gasp.

'What's that?' She was staring at my bracelet.

I held up my wrist. 'This? Oh, it's just a press pass, you know, for when...'

'...A journalist? You're a journalist?'

I nodded.

Her head snapped back as if I'd slapped her, 'You were there to report the trial? You weren't there to support Viktor?'

'Yes...well, no. I was working for my paper, ' I lied. 'But I was always on V's side. You know that, you saw me, every day.' I sounded like a whining brat.

She narrowed her eyes at me. 'Why? Why did you pretend to be his friend - our friend? What sort of a sick bastard does that?'

'Please, Melanie, I wasn't pretending. I wanted to get close to you, to meet you, like I am now. I wanted to help V.'

She stepped away from me. 'Don't you dare call him that', her voice was shrill and I saw her family staring at us. 'Now fuck

145

off. Go write your lies. I thought they were scum,' she screeched, pointing to the reporters, 'but you, you're a bloodsucker. I hope you rot in Hell.' And she hurled the box of truffles in my face.

The lid came off and the sweets scattered everywhere on the shiny floor. For a moment I was unable to move, but then my brain kicked in. 'No!' I yelled. 'No one touch them. They're V's. Leave them.' And I ran, scooping up the sweets as I went, jamming them in my pockets. I got five...six, and saw two more under a chair. I knocked the chair over and grabbed them, then, in the corner of my eye I saw a small child bend down to pick something up and I leapt at him, knocking him away, but there was nothing there. Still two missing. 'Please, please. Give them back to me.' Startled people jumped away as I charged straight through them, searching, searching.

I was on my hands and knees when Dan got to me. He pulled me to my feet and tried to hustle me away but I fought him, clawing at his face. 'Leave me alone,' I sobbed. 'I have to find them.'

He clung on. 'No, no, it's okay. I promise, it's all okay, Evie. Come away.'

I tore myself out of his grasp and ran at the people again but Dan caught me around the waist and swung me off my feet. I wriggled and squirmed and lashed out but he held tight and dragged me backwards across the lobby and through the door. By the time we got outside he was gasping for breath and he dumped

146

me on a low wall, still holding onto my wrists. I kicked him hard but he didn't let go.

'Please. I must find them.' I wailed. 'You don't understand. Someone's going to die and it's all my fault.'

'For God's sake, Evie, keep your voice down. I've got them, I've got the other two. Promise to stay there while I show you? Promise?'

But I wasn't listening. 'They're innocent and they're going to die.'

'Look,' he yelled, thrusting his hand in his pocket and shoving what he was holding in front of my nose. I was staring down at the two missing sweets. 'Ten to a box.' Dan said, letting me go and sinking down onto the wall beside me. He was breathing heavily. 'Thank God you're pernickety.'

I couldn't take my eyes off those last two truffles. I don't know how long we sat like that, but eventually I looked at Dan. There was a long scratch down his cheek. It was bleeding.

I touched his face and he flinched. 'Sorry,' I whispered.

'Could have been worse. I might have eaten one of these little beauties.' And he held up a truffle.

'Be careful.'

'Oh, I am, believe me.' He put the sweet in his pocket. 'I knew you were going to do something but I never imagined this. ' He shook his head slowly. 'Unbelievable. What in God's name possessed you to try a trick like this?'

'I had to. I promised her.'

147

Dan stood up and held out his hands. 'Give them to me.'

I couldn't move, so he took the truffles out of my pockets 'Right, there's a loo over the road. See?' He pulled me up beside him. My legs were shaking so much I could hardly stand and he helped me across the street. He made me go in the Ladies to wash my hands while he flushed the truffles down the toilet.

When we were done he led me back towards the city centre and found a small park with benches bordering a square of grass. There were families picnicking. We lay down on the grass and I closed my eyes. It was still hot when I woke but the sun was low in the sky. Dan was propped up on one elbow beside me looking down at me. We were under a jacaranda tree in full bloom giving us shade, scattering us with vivid blue blossoms.

Dan flicked a petal out of my hair. 'Were you really going to do it?'

'I don't know. If he'd been well enough to eat them, maybe, but I hadn't thought about the others. I'm so relieved. God, I'm so relieved. I was sure that little kid was going to eat one. I might have murdered a child. Or any of those people - Melanie, or her family. But I've failed. I've let Shon down.'

Dan took my hand. 'Viktor Heiney isn't Nick Ground. Whatever he's done. He isn't the man who murdered Shon.'

'You don't understand. Shon was my life. I owe her everything.'

148

'I didn't know her, Evie, but from what I hear Shon was one of the good guys, a compassionate, forgiving woman and she would want you to live your life. That's what you owe her. Be happy, make her proud.'

'But I made a promise.'

'Come on. D'you really think she would want you to kill someone, anyone, to avenge her death? I don't think so and nor do you, not really.'

The park was empty now and fairy lights flickered in the trees. It was so quiet but in the distance we could hear drums beating. The Carnival was getting close.

Dan helped me up and we walked hand in hand out of the park and onto the street.

'I didn't think you'd come back, Dan. I thought I'd lost you too.'

'Where would I go?

'Did he...?'

'...Yeah, before I got there, but it's okay, no need to look so tragic. There was nothing I could have done or said. Words don't always cover it do they?' And he took my face in his hands and gave me such a calm, loving look before kissing me gently on the lips.

Later that night when the street parades were over and the crowds and noise and beat of the drums had melted away into the warm darkness, we went to find Dan's car.

149

'Gave up on the bike,' he confessed. 'Got to learn to accept my external parameters - read all about that in the in-flight magazine on the plane - got to know when to stop running.'

As we got in the car I said, 'I'm messed up, Dan. I think I always will be.'

He didn't say anything but I saw his expression in the headlights of a passing car. He looked so serious. And I knew he didn't want me. How could he? What sane person would choose to hang around with a crazy like me?

'Could you drop me off somewhere?'

'Sure. The station okay?'

'I...er...yeah.'

'That was a joke, Evie. D'you remember them? '

'I don't know what you want from me, Dan, but I haven't got much to give.'

'That's okay,' he said. 'I don't want much, just a pernickety, violent, beautiful woman called Evie Adze.'

Had he said that? Had he said beautiful? I didn't know what came next, so I said the first thing that popped into my head. 'But I haven't got a job.'

He laughed out loud. 'We'll find you one.'

'And I haven't got a home.'

'Ditto.'

He started the engine and pulled away from the kerb.

'Where are we going, Dan?'

He thought for a moment, then he grinned. 'What about the beach? I know the perfect spot. Oh, and there's one other thing I need to tell you.'

I started to say something but he put his finger to his lips. . 'Shh, just listen, okay? Are you ready?'

I nodded.

'I've found him, Evie.'

'What?'

'I've found him. I know where Nick Ground is.'

About the Author

Anne Ousby lives on the Northumbrian Coast in England. She is a playwright, short story writer and, more recently, a novelist. Her stories have been published in anthologies and on radio. Her stage plays have been performed widely in the North East and her television drama, 'Wait till the Summer Comes', was broadcast on !TV.

'Patterson's Curse' p 2010 Roomtowrite www.roomtowrite.co.uk

'The Leopard Man' p 2012.

'The Last Iceberg' Sci-Fi p 2012

'Your Friend E' is her third novel set in contemporary South Africa inspired by frequent visits to the Western Cape, where her family live.

Glossary

Kugals - over-groomed materialistic women

braai - barbecue

wors - sausage

potjie pot - caste-iron cooking pot

rooibus - red bush tea

bakkie - pick-up truck

stoep - porch/veranda

dagga - marijuana

kif - cool, great, wicked

Made in the USA
Charleston, SC
22 July 2015